WRAPPED UP IN YOU

MILLER FAMILY MEDICAL
BOOK 2

DAPHNE JAMES HUFF

Miller Family
MEDICAL ROMANCE

Miller Family
MEDICAL ROMANCE

Wrapped Up in You

DAPHNE JAMES HUFF

For all those who've been through the worst and felt like they could never tell anybody about it.

ONE

BASTIEN

The giant smile on Bastien's face was so wide, his jaw ached.

This was good news, he reminded himself. His twin sister and his best friend were getting married. In three months.

He needed to get out of this dining room.

"Congratulations." The single, flat word, as hollow as his chest, was drowned out by the enthusiastic clamor around the long dining room table. Nobody noticed the tight grip he had on his fork, or the noise it made when he let go and it dropped onto his plate. He was surrounded by his family, and had never been so lonely.

"Is this why you insisted I drive up even though I have an early class tomorrow?" His younger sister Clementine's face split into a wide grin, which softened her grumpy words. As did the giant hug she wrapped Anais in seconds later.

Bastien held back an eye roll. Of course his twin would badger Clementine about this.

Anais's voice was muffled as she returned the embrace. "I know I wasn't exactly thrilled when you said you were going to get your DPT and not MD, but that doesn't mean I don't want you in the wedding."

Suspicions confirmed. The big bombshell of Clementine going into physical therapy instead of general medicine hadn't been in Anais's five-year plan for the family medical clinic she ran with their dad, so naturally she'd freaked out. Now she'd decided it was all in the past so that her wedding could be the perfect event she wanted. He leaned back in his chair and crossed his arms. It was like he knew Anais even better than himself.

So why didn't I see this coming?

Everyone was crowded around the happy couple, doling out handshakes and hugs like they were manning the candy booth at the town's Halloween Festival, while Bastien stayed rooted in his chair, pulse racing and face heating.

"I'll go get champagne." Before anyone could respond, he was out of his seat, through the kitchen, and down the stairs to the basement. The cool, carpeted space was full of worn furniture and more books than a university library.

Letting out a shaky exhale, he leaned his head against a bookshelf.

"I'm happy for them," he whispered to the dozens of copies of old textbooks his parents had kept all these years. "This is a good thing."

Maybe if he said it enough, he'd believe it.

"Is everything okay?" At the sound of Anais's voice behind him, he turned to find his twin giving him her patented beady-eyed, oldest-sister-by-thirteen-minutes stare. The one that he, even less than the others, could never lie to. She'd see right through him, just like she had when he'd escaped down here.

That didn't mean he was going to make it easy on her.

"Everything's fine." He straightened up and made his way to the wine racks in one corner of the finished basement.

Anais clicked her tongue impatiently. "So why are you down here sulking?"

"I'm not sulking," he said, as sulkily as he could. He grabbed the bottle directly in front of him. "I'm getting champagne to celebrate."

"I understand if you're feeling jealous—"

"I'm not jealous," he said hotly, but it wasn't entirely true.

Jealousy was absolutely one of the emotions coursing through him, heating his blood and blurring his vision. After all, it wasn't just that his friend had gotten to this milestone first. His twin sister, who already got everything first and did everything right, was getting it too.

Rising above all that, however, was a deep, aching sense of loneliness. Every bone was lead while his body floated empty above the carpet.

"I'm just amazed you're rushing this."

Anais blinked and shook her head, surprised, for once, by something Bastien said.

"What rush? I've been with Jackson for over a year and a half."

"That's not even half as long as I've known him." Bastien's chest filled with a hot, angry energy that he knew had nothing to do with Jackson or Anais, but since she was the one here, he'd take it out on her. "Not even a third."

She put her hands on her hips and glared at him again. "Is there some reason I shouldn't marry him that you haven't told me?"

As quickly as it had risen, the heat fell away. He turned his head at a sharp burst of muffled laughter from upstairs, where everyone was still celebrating the happy news. He looked back at his sister, whose questioning glare hadn't shifted.

"Of course not. Jackson's great."

His friend since college, Jackson had been there for Bastien when his life had fallen apart—twice. Bastien had returned the favor when Jackson's parents had disowned him for choosing baseball over a career in medicine like they wanted.

It was something Bastien could relate to: the only one in his family to not be a doctor, picking sports over medicine. One important difference, however, would forever separate the friends.

Jackson had spent a decade in the pros while Bastien's junior-year injury had literally shattered his major league soccer dreams.

Now Jackson was getting the ultimate happy ending. A life with a woman he loved. Bastien's hand tightened around the bottle, and he stepped away from the wine rack.

He'd never have the same. He didn't deserve that kind of happiness, not after failing everyone so badly.

"If he's so great, what's the problem?" Anais picked up a bottle and switched it for the one in Bastien's hand.

"There's not enough time." He took back his original bottle, swiping at the dust on the label so he could read the name. Of course it was a good one. If there was one thing Dr. Heather Miller knew better than the radiology she specialized in, it was French wine. "August fifteenth isn't even three months from now. You know that's less time than the average high school soccer season?"

"It's the only week Minnie has a break in her accelerated program, and, well..." There was a slight tinge of red in Anais's cheeks as she looked away and ran her hand along the top of the wine rack. She adjusted several bottles so the labels were all facing in the same direction. "I know it's silly, age is just a number, blah, blah, blah. But I want to get married before I turn thirty."

Her eyes didn't quite meet his. He inhaled sharply and shifted his body away from her, just a little. Not enough to upset her, but enough for her to know her words hurt him.

"Which is the same day I'll turn thirty." The age he would have retired from soccer, once upon a time.

Anais tucked her hair behind her ear, eyes still on the wine rack. "You know it's not the same for guys."

No, it wasn't. Nothing was the same between him and Anais besides their eye color. His long, slow inhale did little to ease the familiar aching isolation that swelled in his chest. She was so close to having everything she wanted while he was still playing catch-up. He fiddled with the metal cage on the top of the champagne bottle, digging it into his thumb, the bite of it keeping him grounded when he felt like he might drift away.

It was ridiculous to feel that kind of solitude in a family of five kids. But ever since his three younger siblings had all left for school, and Anais had found Jackson, he felt like the only one not moving forward in his life.

With a flip of her hair, Anais broke the awkward silence. "Besides, did you really think I'd want some huge wedding that would take a year to plan?"

"Well, yeah." Bastien gestured to her perfection. Not a hair out of place, her clothes perfectly coordinated, even for a casual family dinner. "You love to plan. I know this year has been hard for you, not knowing what would happen with Jackson's baseball contract."

If she knew him well, he knew her just as well. The unpredictability of a baseball player's life, especially one at the tail end of his career like Jackson, had been difficult for his sister, even if she wouldn't admit it.

"It has been hard."

His eyebrows shot up. Maybe she would admit it.

Who is this person, and what's she done with Anais?

Ignoring his bemused expression, she shrugged, her dark hair shining in the low light and shadows dancing across her face. "After the year we've had, I really want to do something fun and happy this summer."

He understood the feeling, but he also knew his sister. "You sure it'll be fun and not more stress for you?"

"Are you saying you'd like to help plan the wedding?" The corner of her lip twitched.

He stood up straighter and his chest puffed out. Finally, a way to be useful to her. "If you need me to."

Whether it was covering a class for a fellow teacher, extra coaching for a player with potential, helping a friend move, or running yet another festival in the town center, everyone counted on Bastien to help. He'd do anything for his sister, for his family, for the town. Anais knew that better than anyone and was usually the one to push back, telling him he was doing too much.

But it would never be too much. He'd never be enough. His selfish reaction to Anais's news proved that. Rather than congratulating them like they deserved, he'd run away like a sullen teenager who'd been cut from varsity.

Her head tilted and her lips pursed together like she was actually considering it. "I think it'll be fine, but I'll let you know if that changes."

"Really?" Eager anticipation shot through him as he tried to keep the hope out of his voice. Another chance to help, another chance to make himself useful.

"Really, Bibi." When she punched his arm along with using the horrible nickname only she used, he knew she meant it. "Now can we please go back upstairs so we can celebrate this?"

Before they did, he pulled her into a hug. "Thank you. I've always thought of him as a brother, and now he really will be."

"Yes, because this was all for you." The sarcasm was thick in her voice, but she still squeezed him back.

Bastien followed her up the stairs, her words sinking down slowly in his chest like a rock falling into the creek. In all areas of his life—brother, teacher, coach, friend, volunteer—he was used to thinking of others. In a family of doctors, he needed to give back in a way as significant as what they did.

But just once, it would be nice for her words to be true. For something to be all for him. Tonight, though, it was all about Anais, and he would be there for her, like he always would be.

———

Three bottles of celebratory champagne later, Bastien had won the Miller family's game night with his usual underhanded methods, and everyone was laughing. The air was bubbling with joy, and his cheeks hurt from smiling so much. The evening was ending much better than it had started.

"Well, it seems this is the night for news." Bastien's dad put down his glass, and a serious look spread over his face. Not quite sad, but almost.

That was all it took to get Bastien's heart racing. Imagining all the worst-case scenarios for his dad's somber expression, he shot a glance at Anais. Her lips turned down, which only increased the unevenness of his pulse. If it was the retirement they'd all been pushing him to take for years, he would've discussed it with Anais first. Whatever this was, it was news to her as well.

He didn't even bother checking his mom's face. He'd get zero help there. Their mom's expression would be infuriatingly blank, the way it always was when serious topics came up.

"I've decided to sell the old Miller cabin." His dad settled back in his chair. "The town approached me about it a few weeks ago about buying the land, and I think it's time."

Bastien let out a strangled sound, his heart in his throat. "You can't sell," he said, his heart pounding. "It's our history."

Everyone turned to stare at Bastien, different levels of surprise on their faces.

Was his response really that shocking? He stared back at them all, his hands balled into fists on either side of his plate. "The Millers have been doctors here since the eighteen nineties. That cabin is part of our family's story, the town's history."

This was even worse than their dad retiring. At least when he did that, there'd be Anais and eventually Danielle and Elias to continue the legacy. Even Clementine was ensuring, in her own way, there'd always be Millers taking care of people in Jasper Creek. Bastien wasn't a part of that legacy, as useless as the old cabin, but that didn't mean he wanted to see it sold and likely torn down.

"It's a total wreck, Bastien, and has been since the sixties." Anais folded her arms across her chest. "Honestly, I don't know why Dad hasn't sold it before this. That's prime real estate on the edge of town, right on all the trails."

"Maybe they'll make a park out of it." Elias leaned forward in his chair, the eighteen-year-old eager for a chance to chime in like one of the grown-ups. "The town needs more green."

More green? The air vibrated around Bastien's head. They were surrounded by the mountains. Amazing hiking and skiing were less than twenty minutes away.

Bastien tried and failed to keep the anger out of his voice. "The town needs to respect its history and everything the Millers have done for them."

There was a round of groans and eye rolling from everyone. The only person not looking at him like he was a new kind of disease to be eradicated was his dad, whose contemplative eyes held a familiar glimmer.

"What did you have in mind?" he asked.

The air left Bastien's lungs in a whoosh. "What do you mean?"

"I haven't signed anything." His dad leaned back, eyes intense and hands folded in front of him. "It was just one conversation. What would you do with the cabin?"

Possibilities filtered through his mind at a rapid-fire pace while his heart beat a staccato rhythm in his ears. After a few moments of tapping his fingers on the table in time to his pulse, he picked the first idea that seemed halfway feasible. "I could fix it up."

"And do what with it?"

His dad was doing the thing he always had. Just because Bastien wasn't a science major or going into medicine didn't mean he shouldn't be as thoughtful and methodical as his siblings. Bastien took a deep breath at the reminder, his chest puffing a little at the subtle pride this kind of attention gave him. Precision and analysis were what had made him a good soccer player. And what made him a good coach and history teacher now.

"If it's fixed up, maybe the town would want to use it as a museum."

"There's already a museum for the town," Anais said with a huff.

Bastien bit his tongue to avoid sticking it out at her.

"Then you could sell it as a home. You'd get more for it." He knew it wasn't about the money, but his father scratched his chin.

"I like the idea of someone living there again. None of you kids would want to live in it?"

There were vigorous shaking heads all around the table. Hope flitted through Bastien's chest and he clung to it, as desperately as a man in a raging river held tight to a floating log.

This was exactly what he needed right now. Saving the Miller cabin from demolition was something big, something to prove he could contribute to the family and their legacy in a meaningful way.

"You'd have to finish up before the wedding." From her seat across the table, his mom finally spoke up. "I know school's almost over, but you already have a lot to do this summer. There are the sport camps you run and the town's Fourth of July Festival, which is already too much. How are you going to find the time to work on the house on top of all that?"

Just like they always did, his mom's reasonable and practical words ripped his hope away.

"I'll figure it out." Seven pairs of eyes bore into him, and he lifted his chin high. "This is important. To me, to the Millers, to this town."

"I had no idea this mattered so much to you." His dad's eyes were shining. Mostly from four glasses of champagne, but Bastien saw some pride mixed in there too.

Ignoring her husband, his mom raised an eyebrow at him. "Have you been out there lately? It's a mess."

Excitement strummed in Bastien's veins now that he knew his dad was leaning toward saying yes, and he waved away his mother's concern.

"I did all the work on my house, besides the electricity and plumbing." Bastien's fingers danced along the edge of the table, eager to get started on a new project. "I turn town square into a Halloween Festival and winter wonderland every year. I can handle turning a three-room cabin into something sellable."

His mom pursed her lips and raised an eyebrow, a mirror image of her other children. Meanwhile, Jackson was shaking his head and smirking, knowing perfectly well he'd get dragged into this at some point, the same way he had for every town event Bastien ran. For now, his friend stayed silent, probably not wanting to upset his fiancée so early in their engagement.

"It was already renovated in the seventies, so I just need to update it a little. It won't have to be perfect, just cleaned up enough to make the possibilities visible to the right buyer."

The confidence in his voice would have anyone not related to him thinking he flipped houses for a living instead of teaching teenagers the differences between primary sources and secondary sources. This house was a primary source of Miller family history, and he couldn't let it be torn down without at least trying to save it.

Knowing he'd pay for it later, he decided it was time to drag his best friend into things. "Jackson's helping me with the camps, so I won't be totally on my own this summer. I'll have loads of time."

There was an exchange of glances between the two senior Miller doctors at each end of the table, and when his mom sighed and shook her head, he knew he'd won. He leaned back in his chair, a wide smile on his face and a jittery anticipation thrumming in his veins. Jackson caught his eye and raised his eyebrows as if to ask Bastien if this was what he really wanted to do. He nodded at his friend, using all the restraint he had not to jump from the table and drag him to the hardware store so they could get started right away.

This was exactly what he needed this summer.

TWO

GABBY

"So what did you do this weekend?"

It was a simple question, and Gabby was sure that Jane, her coworker and fellow nurse practitioner, had no idea it would set her heart racing and her palms sweating.

"Nothing much. You?" Gabby flashed a smile that she didn't feel, knowing that the best way to get someone to stop being curious about you was to ask them about themselves.

Jane did not disappoint.

She spent the next ten minutes telling her all about hiking with her friends and going out to eat with her family at a new restaurant in Denver. All Gabby had to do was sip her tea, nod, and murmur "Oh, that sounds nice" every so often. This left her plenty of energy to calm down her pulse that always ticked up a few notches whenever someone asked about her personal life.

She knew what would happen if she told Jane, or anyone, the truth. That she'd spent most of the weekend tutoring high schoolers in science, racking up as many hours as she could because soon it would be the summer and this lucrative source of secondary income would be gone until the fall.

If she told her colleague that this was what she did in her spare time, she'd get a half-impressed nod and comment on how week-ends were for relaxing, then Jane would ask why she needed the money. Gabby would be forced to either lie or bare her soul to someone she hardly knew.

Much safer to have other people talk about themselves.

Just as Jane was winding down her story, Dr. Anais Miller poked her head into the break room.

"Oh great, you're both here." Anais smiled in a distracted sort of way. "Could you meet me here in the break room at eleven? And tell Austin if you see him? I already checked with Hunter, and none of us have appointments then."

"Sure." Jane smiled brightly and stood up, dumping the rest of her morning coffee in the sink like this request was no big deal.

Gabby, however, knew with absolute certainty that it had to be bad news.

As she washed out her own mug and headed out into the hall-way, a vise locked itself around her chest that no amount of belly breathing could loosen. The possibilities were limited but dramatic. They were being bought, or joining a hospital group, something that meant fewer hours and fewer patients. Gabby was the newest, so she'd be the first to be asked to leave. Already mentally going through her contacts, she was miserable at the thought of having to leave the first place she'd really liked working in the five years she'd been an NP.

Instead of the relaxed morning she needed, taking the time to talk to each patient the way she loved, her worry made its way from her chest into her stomach and set up camp. She gritted her teeth through the familiar painful bloating while asking patients far fewer questions than she usually did, escaping as quickly as possible after each appointment so she could do a few stretches in the bathroom. Sometimes that worked to ease the tension in her gut, but she had no luck today.

By the time everyone gathered in the break room, Gabby's heart was beating faster than was technically healthy for someone of her age and weight. A few discreet, calming breaths did nothing to control her raging anxiety, however. Repeating to herself that she'd be fine no matter what happened sort of helped, but her stomach was still twisted into a tight knot.

When they were all squished into the small room, Anais cleared her throat and cast a glance at her father. "Thanks everyone. I just wanted to tell all of you at once."

The blood rushing through Gabby's ears made it hard to hear, even though Anais was barely ten feet away in the cramped space. She peeked at Jane perched on the counter above the mini fridge—impressive considering she was at least two decades older than Gabby—and then glanced at Hunter, the baby-faced receptionist sitting next to her. They'd both stay, having been here long before Gabby had arrived in April. The only other staff member at Miller Family Medical was Dr. Austin Gibson. He was Anais's friend from med school, so there was no way he'd be leaving.

Gabby shifted slightly, turning her head down and slightly away in an attempt to hear better, but also to potentially hide what might be tears in a few moments.

"Jackson and I are getting married this summer!"

Gabby's head shot up and just caught the wide, excited smile on Anais's face before Austin whooped and crushed his friend in a hug. The weight of anxiety lifted from Gabby's shoulders so quickly she was lightheaded in its absence.

This was good news. Happy news.

Any normal person wouldn't have assumed the worst, but Gabby hadn't had a normal upbringing. Expecting the world to fall out from under her had come from experience. Even the past few years of relative calm and success weren't enough to fully let go of the fear she'd grown up with. Gabby had spent most of her adult life preparing for whatever disaster was coming next.

A wedding isn't a disaster. At least, not for people like Anais and Jackson. Gabby had only seen them together a few times, but it was clear they were head over heels for each other. Gabby didn't have many examples of happy couples in her life, but the Millers were definitely a part of that small group.

"Congratulations." Her voice was shaking when it was finally her turn to say something. Hunter asked about wedding dresses, and Jane exclaimed with delight over the engagement ring Anais pulled out on a chain around her neck. Apparently it wasn't sized right, but she didn't want to take it to a jeweler yet.

What should Gabby say? Her stomach twisted again. She hadn't been the kind of girl who'd dreamed of her own wedding, too worried about just surviving her teens to think about what came after. Then through nursing school she'd been laser focused on doing the best she possibly could, no time for dating, even less for thoughts of engagement rings and white dresses.

"Will your family be in the wedding?" There, that was a totally normal thing to ask. "Your sisters will be bridesmaids, right?"

"Oh, I don't know if I'll even do that, it's going to be really small." Anais brushed her dark hair back from her face, elation still shining in her eyes. How had Gabby missed it? Oh right, she'd been freaking out all morning that she was about to lose her job. "You're all invited, of course. But it'll just be a backyard thing like our Easter picnic. Nothing fancy."

Gabby choked back a laugh. The Millers had invited the staff to their Easter picnic in their backyard earlier that spring. The wide lawn had stretched out for acres and had direct access to the picturesque creek the town was named after. Most of the town had been there, in elegant clothes, eating off tiny plates under a giant white tent while Gabby hid her stomach cramps in the one nice dress she owned.

"Nothing fancy" meant something entirely different to the Millers than it did to her.

"I can't wait," Gabby said with a genuine smile.

She liked Anais and was happy for her. Especially now that she knew she wouldn't be unemployed in the near future.

Everyone else expressed the same sentiment, and they all went back to work in a cloud of excited chatter.

Despite how it had started, the rest of the day went well for Gabby. Everyone was in a good mood, and it was hard not to get caught up in the excitement everyone had for Anais. Jasper Creek was a small town, and by the middle of the afternoon, Gabby's patients were abuzz with the news, saying nothing but good things about Jackson.

Thanks to her chatty patients, Gabby knew within hours that he'd been a professional baseball player and was almost done with his teaching degree. While he'd only permanently moved to town six months ago, he was already ingrained in the fabric of the town's life thanks to frequent visits and his general helpfulness.

"He'll be coaching alongside Bastien this summer with all the sports camps the high school runs," said Mrs. Foster while Gabby was checking her blood pressure. The older woman had been chattering nonstop about the happy couple since entering the exam room. "Though I'm sure if wedding planning gets busy, Bastien will pitch in the way he always does."

Gabby's mouth went dry at the mention of Anais's twin brother. She knew firsthand just how helpful he could be, though the memory still filled her with an unfamiliar salty-sweet mix of embarrassment and longing.

"You're all set, Mrs. Foster." Gabby wrapped her stethoscope around her neck and stood up to make a note in the older woman's chart. "Those new meds seem to be doing the trick. Do you need a refill on the prescription?"

"No, I'll be fine, dear. Thank you." She took Gabby's arm to step off the exam table. "It's been lovely having someone who's so focused on women's health."

That had been the big reason she'd been hired by the Millers, Gabby knew that, but it was nice to hear it from the patients as well. While her choice of specialty had more to do with her own family history than she'd like to admit, what she loved was being able to use her knowledge to educate women about their bodies. So many of the mysteries and questions she'd had no one to talk to about when she was young had been answered by some of her first biology classes. She never wanted anyone to feel that confused about their own health. Despite the extra debt it had meant at the time, the choice to continue her studies after nursing school to become an NP had been an easy one.

Gabby led Mrs. Foster back into the reception area, sunny and bright thanks to the giant windows that looked out onto the street. "Well, I'm happy to be here," she said with a smile at the older woman.

She meant it too. A smaller practice came with its own difficulties, as her not-so-mild stress this morning proved, but it was a nice change of pace from hurrying from exam room to exam room in her previous job, always feeling like she had to rush through in the allotted time in order to stay on schedule and budget.

Her own personal budget had been the deciding factor in taking this job. Jasper Creek was a solid forty minutes away—longer whenever her car was having trouble—but it paid more than any job she'd ever had. Every dollar mattered.

After waving goodbye to Mrs. Foster, Gabby popped into the break room to check her phone before her next appointment. There was a message from her roommate.

My boyfriend found a job here finally! I'll need you to move out by the end of the week, okay?

Sinking dread ate away at all the happiness that had built up over the course of the afternoon. It didn't matter that she still had a job because pretty soon she wouldn't have a place to live.

Gabby rushed from the break room before anyone came in and asked her questions. Her face must be a mess of worry, and she hid in the one place she knew she wouldn't be disturbed. The bathroom had a locked door and a chair for her to sit in while she let the panic and despair work its way through her system.

This was entirely her own fault. Living as frugally as possible meant sometimes putting up with atrocious roommates. This one had seemed different, sweet in her ad and in person, so Gabby hadn't thought twice about not signing any kind of lease. Half the time she didn't, taking whatever rooms were cheapest and cleanest.

Looking up into the mirror, she inhaled deeply. "You'll find something else. You always do."

But what if you don't? whispered that nasty little voice that was always there.

There was a knock at the door and Hunter's voice floated in. "Gabby, are you okay? Your next appointment is here."

"I'm fine." She stood up and washed her hands. Her stomach was still churning and her breath was a little unsteady, but the worst of it was over. If Gabby had a patient with two bouts of anxiety in one day that were so bad they interrupted work, what would she do? Probably give her a referral to a mental health professional, but that wasn't something Gabby could afford right now. Once she found a place to live, she'd take a look.

Though she was far from okay, Gabby opened the door with a wide smile for Hunter.

"Thanks for letting me know."

The rest of the day passed in a blur. The second her shift was over, Gabby bid a quick goodbye to Hunter on her way out the door, her phone already in her hand and rental websites pulled up. With her eyes trained on the pitiful offerings in the area, her feet were on autopilot for the short walk to her car.

She swiped past those that were obviously scams, the picture-perfect bedrooms that were probably pulled from a furniture website.

Everything else was either twice as much as she'd been paying her soon-to-be-former roommate or a complete dump. She was used to living in miserable conditions, but it was getting harder to bear now that she was in her early thirties.

By the time she got to the parking lot, her heart was pounding again. A few slow inhales and a reminder that she had a few days before she had to completely panic helped, but just barely.

Then she ran into a brick wall.

She fell to the ground with a loud "oof" and a painful jab to her glutes.

"Yikes, I'm sorry, Gabby. I thought you saw me coming."

Dazed, she looked up to see Bastien Miller's green eyes staring down at her, full of worry, his hand already extended toward her to help her up. "Are you okay?"

In that breathless moment before she took his offered hand, Gabby had the urge to tell him just how not okay she really was. The upward tilt of his eyebrows invited her to blurt out how out of control her stomach pains had been today, how worried she was, how completely messed up her life seemed to be no matter how many good things happened. The worried pucker of his mouth looked like it could hold all of that for her and make it disappear.

"I'm fine." She let him pull her up and then looked around for her phone. A crush of disappointment hit her in the chest when she saw it on the ground next to her car with a giant crack in the screen.

Before she could say or do anything, Bastien bent and picked up her phone, also noticing the screen. He winced. "I'm sorry, I can get that fixed for you. Unless you have insurance that'll take care of it?"

Gabby let out a rueful chuckle. Insurance. Who was she, a Rockefeller? "It's fine." She barely had a phone plan, getting by with the minimum since everywhere she worked and lived had Wi-Fi.

"Looking for a new apartment?" He handed the phone back to her, then met her eye. A slow flush crept across his cheeks. "Sorry, I didn't mean to pry."

She tucked her phone into her pocket. "If you know of anywhere for under six hundred that I can move into this weekend, I'm all ears."

His eyes lit up and her stomach dropped to the ground, her hand frozen in her pocket.

Did I really just say that to him?

She barely knew him, and she worked with his father and sister. This wasn't exactly something she wanted getting back to them.

But he had helped her once before, and he did know a lot of people in the area. Teachers at the high school lived in surrounding towns, so he might know of something.

Yes, that was why she'd told him. It had nothing to do with his gentle expression sending prickles of tenderness up and down her arms. Gabby did not accept help when she was perfectly capable of doing things herself. It felt too much like pity, and she was not someone to be pitied.

He frowned and brushed his hand against the light brown stubble on his chin. "Six hundred?"

"I could go up to eight hundred if I needed to," she said quickly, hoping the desperate tone in her voice wasn't too obvious.

"Maybe you could live at my place."

Gabby's heart almost stopped in her chest. "Excuse me?"

She took a step back. *Do I sound that desperate?*

His eyes widened and he held up his hands, palms out. "I should explain. I'm fixing up the old Miller cabin this summer, and I planned on living there to maximize working time. So my house will be empty."

"Oh." That sounded perfect. Too perfect. A familiar anxious twinge twisted around her gut. "I wouldn't want to impose or anything."

"No imposition. It'll be a big help for me, actually." He smiled at her, and it took her a minute to be able to breathe again. The man had somehow gotten more attractive in the past few minutes. "You can make sure my plants and fish don't die."

"I can do that." Her heart leaped into her throat, making it hard to speak. She'd do whatever he needed. *This is amazing, he's amazing, he's wonderful.*

"Is eight hundred okay?"

"No."

Dread dropped into her stomach. Trying to keep her breathing normal, Gabby quickly did the math in her head. "Of course, it's a good location, you probably want at least—"

"Six hundred is fine."

Gabby shook her head. "You can't do that. It should be a fair price."

"It is a fair price for something I wasn't planning on renting out anyway." He ran a hand through his hair, the light catching on a few of the messy brown strands. "And you'll only be able to stay through the summer. I'll help you look for something else for the fall."

"No, I'll be fine." It would be better than fine. Her hands were shaking so hard she had to ball them into fists at her sides to keep him from noticing. She'd save hundreds on gas if she lived so close to work for three months.

A surge of gratitude flowed out of her in Bastien's direction. "This is such a huge help, you have no idea."

This wasn't just solving her immediate problem. It was getting her even closer to her dream.

A home of her own.

She smiled at him, trying to put every ounce of appreciation she could into her voice. "I owe you huge."

Something flickered in his eyes, but before Gabby could catch what it might mean, his expression cleared and the typical smile she always saw on Bastien's face was back.

"You'll just owe me rent. That's enough." He glanced toward the entrance to the clinic, then held out his phone. "I have to meet my dad, but give me your number and we'll figure out a time to meet up and figure out the details."

The happiness and relief were so palpable, Gabby was

tempted to hug him when she handed him his phone. But she held back, reminding herself that if it wasn't appropriate to hug her boss's son, then it would be super inappropriate to hug her landlord.

"See you soon." He gave her a little wave and headed into the building, leaving her in the parking lot next to her car with a chest full of what felt like helium balloons.

During the long drive back to what would soon be her former apartment, she knew she should be focusing on the practical side of things. Figuring out exactly how much she'd be able to save or thinking about finding some tutoring jobs in Jasper Creek for the summer. Worrying about how to make sure this didn't endanger her position at Miller Family Medical in any way.

Instead, she wondered what it would have felt like to have hugged Bastien.

THREE

BASTIEN

The cabin was—just like his mom had said—a mess.

According to Nolan, a contractor who worked for the town on most big projects, it was worse than a mess.

"It would be simpler to just knock it down and build something new." The older man shook his silver-haired head as he walked through with Bastien at his side.

It was early Saturday morning, the day after school ended. Bastien had the keys for a few days now and had visited twice to brainstorm ideas, but this was the first time he'd gotten a professional's take on the project.

The professional did not sound too positive. "I'm seeing rot everywhere, and I doubt the electric and plumbing is up to code. No one's lived here since the seventies, right?"

"The eighties." A small tendril of worry wrapped itself around Bastien's throat and squeezed as he looked around the tiny front room. His car was filled with stuff he thought he'd be moving in to the cabin today. When he'd been through with his dad a few days ago, it had just looked dirty and dusty. Not rotting.

The enthusiasm he'd had then, the energy his dad had loved and shared, felt like pure idiocy now. Working on his own house, built in the nineties, and on town projects, hadn't prepared him for something like this.

He cleared his throat and rubbed the back of his neck. "My aunt was the last one to live here before she moved out to the farm."

The small, three-room cabin had served as a kind of crash pad for the various Miller family members over the years. A bedroom barely big enough for a bed, a living room that was mostly filled with a wood-burning stove, and a minuscule kitchen was all there was, but it was all that Millers needed when they were starting out. Just more proof of how important the cabin was to their family. He had to save it. If that meant a little more work than he'd planned, well, so be it.

"Doesn't look like she did much to it." Nolan kicked at a pile of leaves in the corner, and a scurry of noise and fur streaked out of it. "Nature's started to take over again."

"You don't think anything can be saved?"

"Oh, you can do whatever you want with enough time and money." After poking at a few spots on an exterior wall, it gave way easily to Nolan's fingers. Bastien's stomach dropped to the leaf-covered floor as the walls literally crumbled before his eyes. "The most important thing here is the roof. It's how the water got in."

"Okay, a new roof." That didn't sound impossible. It was a small roof. Bastien ran an eager hand along the edge of a flaking windowsill. "What else?"

Nolan raised an eyebrow at him. "I know you're pretty handy, but I don't think this is something you can do on your own."

"I won't be alone. Jackson'll lend a hand. And I was planning on bringing in a plumber and electrician out next week."

Nolan nodded, his face visibly relaxing, but then he sighed and put a strong, weathered hand on Bastien's shoulder. "I'd help if I had the time, but I've already got my guys replacing the HVAC at the middle school and the floors at the high school."

Bastien returned the older man's shoulder slap with one of his own. "Don't worry about it. I'll figure it out." Other than Jackson, Bastien hadn't planned on needing anyone else for this. This was his project, his family history. It was up to him to do it.

"Besides the roof and the rot, what else do I need to take care of to get this in sellable shape?"

"New windows and floors. A new kitchen and bathroom. You're really talking about a complete renovation."

"It's a small space though. Would twelve weeks be enough?"

By the tightness in Nolan's mouth, Bastien could already tell the answer would be no. "It would be tricky. Is this a wedding present or something for Anais?"

Bastien bit the inside of his cheek. It was no surprise Nolan already knew the news. Between Carl at the café and the patients at the clinic, everyone in town was gabbing about it at this point. Before too long, her plans for a small, backyard wedding would likely morph into something to include as many people as possible. "Not exactly. I just need to have it done by then."

"It'll be a seven-days-per-week kind of job, and it would cost more than you probably want to spend, but it wouldn't be totally impossible."

That was all Bastien needed to hear to get the little spark of hope back. His mouth spread wide into a grin and his heart soared.

Money wouldn't be an issue. His dad had already agreed to a small budget for improvements, though he'd been thinking it would just be for painting and chopping down some trees. Bastien could cover the rest. Between the scholarship that had put him through college, living at home his first few years after graduating, and his parents helping him with the down payment for his own house, he had more than enough saved up.

There was a twist deep in his gut when he remembered what the money had originally been for.

His own wedding that never happened.

Everyone had told him to do something fun with it when Brenda left. Go on an around-the-world trip or buy some ridiculously impractical car. Instead, the money had just been sitting in the bank, waiting for something that would mean as much to Bastien as the life he'd never have.

"Thanks, Nolan. Can I call you if I have questions?"

"Sure. Can't guarantee I know the answers, but I'm always happy to help you if I can."

"You've already helped more than you realize."

The fire that had been sparked at family game night was now growing into a proper inferno of intention inside him. He had the money, a professional said it wasn't totally impossible, and Bastien was already planning on living here for the summer. Any time he wasn't at the sports camps, he could be working on the house. Jackson wouldn't be as available since he had wedding planning, but that was fine. Bastien could do most of it on his own.

He walked the older man outside to his truck. Nolan cast a glance at the back seat of Bastien's car full of boxes and turned to him with wide eyes. "Were you planning on moving in?"

"Is that not a good idea?" He tried not to let the worry show in his voice. If he couldn't live here, then he'd have to go back on his promise to help Gabby.

The newest staff member at Miller Family Medical had been on Bastien's mind all week. She'd been so distracted when she ran into him, her blond hair pulled back in a tight bun, her dark brown eyes fixed on her phone like her world was falling apart. He'd only seen that look on her face one other time, and he hadn't hesitated to help her then.

Though that had been nothing compared to this. Giving her a place to stay felt like the right thing to do, but maybe it was too much. Just like this whole cabin project probably was, but there was no going back now.

Gabby was so happy when he made the offer. It filled him with that familiar lift in the center of his rib cage that came from knowing he could make someone's life easier, make their day brighter. Her dark eyes had lit up, her face radiating gratitude and joy. His chest swelled even now just remembering how happy she'd been.

Nolan looked the opposite of happy. "Only if you don't want mice and ants as your bedmates who eat all your stuff."

Disappointment flooded him, and he leaned against his car for support. Of course, he wouldn't be able to live at the cabin like he'd been planning.

Gabby was meeting him at his house in a few hours. There was no way he'd be sending her a message to tell her not to come, no way he'd take away her joy. The idea upset him more than the possibility the cabin might not be savable. The potential for her unhappiness and disappointment sat there, deep in his belly, shredding his guts.

"I'm a native Coloradan. I'll camp in the yard." He'd been camping since before he could walk. Living in a tent for a few weeks in the summer wouldn't be a problem.

The look on Nolan's face could only be described as humorously incredulous. "I mean, if you really want to maximize your time working on the house, I guess that makes sense... Just promise me you won't live in the house, okay? It's not safe."

"I promise."

He had absolutely not been planning on living at the cabin when he'd told Gabby she could rent his spare room, but he'd wanted her to take his offer. Needed her to. Something hot and selfish made it impossible for him to let her live anywhere else than his house, even if he knew at least two teachers who had the space.

She would never have said yes if he was living there too. The lines were already so blurred in Jasper Creek between family, friends, and town. Having his father's employee and sister's coworker living with him felt like one step too far.

He hadn't told his family about the arrangement. It was his house, so he could do what he wanted with it. The guest room he'd spent so long getting just right had been used so little over the years. Jackson had only used it during his first visit, then every other time he'd been there he'd stayed with Anais. Dani would crash there sometimes after a party, but that had stopped once she'd gotten serious about her schoolwork and applying to med school.

As he waved at Nolan driving away, he looked back at the cabin, half-hidden behind the overgrown lawn and dangerously drooping trees. He knew exactly why he hadn't told his family about Gabby moving in. He didn't want them to tell him, yet again, that he did too much, that something was a bad idea. Not when he knew it was the right choice. He felt this in the core of his very being, even more than he knew restoring the Miller cabin was the right thing to do.

Though if you asked Nolan, the right choice was knocking the whole thing down.

He glanced at his watch. There wasn't time to worry about that right now. He had to get back to his place to clean it up for Gabby.

When he hopped in the car, instead of turning left to head to his house, he turned right and headed to the giant superstore a few towns over he knew would be open this early. There should still be time to pick up a few things. Even if Bastien wouldn't be there this summer, he wanted her to feel at home.

That's what a good landlord would do, wasn't it?

FOUR
GABBY

Gabby wasn't sure if she wanted to cry, scream, or run away.

This wasn't a normal reaction to someone helping her move. She knew that. But she'd been expecting Bastien to show up with the keys, walk her around the apartment, then leave. She'd expected him to act like every other person she'd ever rented a room from over the past ten years. Or she'd at least expected him to believe her "I've got this" when he asked if she needed help with her fewer than a dozen boxes.

Instead, he'd picked up a box labeled "kitchen" which actually held her hair dryer and five books she couldn't fit anywhere else, and took it straight into the kitchen. The swirling, twisting snarl in her chest was definitely due to some combination of anger and frustration, and had absolutely nothing to do with how his biceps flexed as he carried the box.

"I really don't need help." She set down her box on the counter —labeled "textbooks" but actually full of mugs and tea—and crossed her arms. "I've moved at least fifteen times on my own." Using the same falling-apart boxes every time, but he didn't need to know that.

"I've only moved three times." He patted the top of the box he set down on top of hers and nodded proudly like he'd just built the pyramids himself. "But I've helped people move hundreds of times."

A smile tickled at the edges of her lips. It was easy to imagine him stopping on the side of the road wherever there was a moving van and offering his muscles to strangers. Those same muscles were helping her right now, and she was trying to remember that she wasn't happy about it.

"Only three?"

He nodded and leaned back against the counter, looking totally at ease. Which made sense, since this was his kitchen.

"From my parents' house to college, then back to their house, and finally to this house."

Her eyes danced across the white marble countertops and shiny chrome fixtures, the fridge she knew would be fully stocked, and the window overlooking the big backyard. With a long, slow inhale, Gabby kept an unending wave of jealousy from overwhelming her. It was everything she'd ever wanted, and he didn't even realize how lucky he was.

She wasn't mad at him though. It wasn't like he could know what something as simple as not moving every six months would mean to someone like her. He wasn't bragging, just answering her question.

Putting one hand on the "kitchen" box of non-kitchen items, she pulled at the end of her ponytail with the other. Even on her days off from work, she kept it pulled back, hiding the split ends and lack of hairstyle that came from only going to get it cut when she absolutely had to. "That sounds nice."

"Nice?" The corner of his lip lifted and he tilted his head, like he'd never really thought about it. "Compared to everyone else in my family, it's boring. Anais lived in Seattle for her residency, my dad did a fellowship in Boston, and Jackson's been all over with baseball."

There was a tinge of bitterness to his voice that tugged at her curiosity. She realized she didn't know much about Bastien, but she didn't need to. Not if he was only going to be her landlord for the summer.

Which was why the sudden compulsion to tell him everywhere she'd ever lived, and why, was so frightening.

"Well, I don't mind boring, and I think it's nice to have roots." She picked up the box. "I'll just put this away."

"I've got it." He reached out his arms and her throat locked up. The urge to run into them was overwhelming.

"It's fine," she managed to squeak out.

Hurrying from the kitchen, she silently counted to ten in a vain attempt to calm her racing heart. Whatever attraction she felt toward him, however nice it was to look at his muscles and enjoy seeing him using them for her, it could never be anything more.

The bedroom was small but neat, furnished with a comfortable chair in the corner, a desk with a supportive chair, and a queen bed that he'd put fresh sheets on, even though she'd of course brought her own. It was nicer than anywhere she'd stayed before. Her knees trembled as she put a hand on the desk to steady herself.

An entire house, just for her. It was something she'd never even allowed herself to dream of. The home she was saving so diligently for would be an apartment, something small, and she knew it wouldn't be anywhere near Jasper Creek.

She took a deep breath and ran her hand over the bedspread, the worn cotton softer than the old sheets she had packed away in one of the boxes still in the car. Next to the bed was a small table with a lamp and digital alarm clock that both looked new. She flipped over the clock and saw a sticker. The lamp had a similar one.

Her breath hitched. He'd bought these for her, knowing she'd move in. Well, that wouldn't do. She'd agreed to rent a room and pay him for it, not have him spend money on her. Helping her was one thing, but things were getting too close to pity, and that's the last thing she ever wanted. She wasn't a victim. She wasn't weak.

Everything she'd done to distance herself from her rough early start was proof of that. She was smart. She survived. And she did it on her own, without anyone buying her lamps and clocks.

When she walked out of her room, the offending items in her hands, he'd already brought in all the rest of her boxes and stacked them neatly in the living room.

She let gratitude well inside of her, just for a moment, like a sticky-sweet treat she was indulging in even though she knew it would hurt her stomach later.

"I already have a lamp and alarm clock." She held them out and waved them at him. He pursed his lips as he took the items from her, clearly wanting to argue with her but holding back.

"Thank you for bringing in the rest of the boxes," she said with another tug at the end of her hair. "You didn't have to do that."

"Is this all you have?"

Gabby's cheeks heated. She looked down and tapped each box as if she were counting them, but she knew they were all there. "Yeah. I don't need much."

"I mean, you've got a lamp and clock, so you're all set."

Her gaze shot up to see the ghost of a smile on his face and his green eyes sparkling. Her own mouth turned up.

"I'm sorry if I overstepped," he said. "You probably didn't really need my help for this."

"Probably not, but it was nice of you to offer."

"It's no problem at all."

These words sparked a memory for Gabby of the first time Bastien had helped her, and the breath left her body.

After the Easter picnic at the Millers', her car wouldn't start. She'd sat there for twenty minutes, debating if she should go back in and ask for help, when Bastien had walked past and seen her sitting there. Without even breaking a sweat, he'd been able to get her car started in minutes.

They'd never spoken about it after that, but it was clearly still on his mind as well.

"Is your car doing okay?" His eyes drifted to the window, where they could see her car parked in the driveway.

"It's fine." The heat in her cheeks had reached feverish levels.

Why was he still here? There were no more boxes, she had the keys, what else was there?

"It's only a fifteen-minute walk to the clinic from here." Bastien ran a hand along the edge of a side table like he was checking for lint. Like this wasn't the cleanest, tidiest place she'd ever lived.

"That close?" She tapped her fingers against the top box in the small stack. "That's good to know. Thanks for your help."

"It's you who's helping me." He moved toward the aquarium in the corner of the room. "I need to show you what to do for the fish and plants."

"Oh, of course." That's right, she was getting a good deal on the room since she was also house-sitting.

With a dramatic wave of his arm, he stepped up to the large fish tank filled with a pirate ship and more plants than water. "This is George and Michael."

"George Michael?" Moving closer to the tank and its adorable owner, Gabby bit her lip, trying not to smile.

"Hey, I didn't name them, the kindergartners did."

"Why do you have the kindergartners' fish?" She bent down to peer through the waving plants at the two specks of orange wriggling through the holes in the pirate ship.

"They get new ones every year, and usually a parent takes them. A few years ago, no one volunteered."

"So George and Michael needed somewhere to stay and you offered your home?" Somewhere in the depths of her chest, she was aware of her heart melting. "Sounds familiar."

Pink streaked across his face, and he turned to grab the food from the shelf next to the tank. "If I'm in a position to help someone, I do it. Is that bad?"

"Not unless they don't want help."

He turned his head quickly, his eyes fixed on hers, searching.

She took a step back, the taut lines of his body and intensity of his gaze again giving her that urge again to tell him everything.

"Everyone needs help sometimes."

She cleared her throat. "I like helping people too. But I'm a nurse. Sometimes people will destroy their lives no matter how much help they have."

His eyebrow shot up, curiosity etched into the lines between his eyes and the downward tilt of his mouth.

Too much. She'd said too much. The pity was coming. She could feel it like a wave, pulling at her ankles and lulling her into a sense of security before engulfing her completely.

"But fish will be no problem, I'm sure." She bared her teeth at him in the widest smile she could manage.

Learning one hand on the edge of the console with the tank, he held out the brightly colored fish-food canister.

"Here's their food. It's just a little every other day."

The brush of his hand on hers when she took the food sent hot, little stabbing pinpricks of awareness across her skin.

She nodded, then turned her gaze to the tank. The sunlight threw sparkles across the water, and little rainbows danced around Bastien's feet. "I think I can handle that."

"Now the plants will be a little more complicated..."

There were several different types in his house, and they each had specific watering needs. The longer he talked, the more adorable he got.

"I'm sorry for being so detailed." He was standing next to a giant banana plant, his hand on a branch like a proud father after explaining how to rotate it so it got the best sun during the day. "I know they're just plants, not people, but a few years ago a student gave me one as a gift, and things just spiraled from there."

"You're a natural caregiver, Bastien Miller."

Red flushed his cheeks, making his eyes glow greener than the plants he clearly loved. "No, that's all the other Millers. I just like plants."

He did a lot more than that, but Gabby was dangerously close to saying something she'd regret. It was a very good thing Bastien wouldn't be living here this summer.

She rubbed a hand along one of the banana plant's enormous leaves. It was smoother and waxier than she'd expected.

"Well, I'll do my best to make sure they survive my black thumb." The terror that flashed across his face was so dramatic, she let go of the leaf and laughed. "I'm joking. I like plants too. Just never lived somewhere long enough to get one for myself."

They walked down the creaky stairs back into the large, sunlit living room. Gabby was itching for him to leave, to have the space to herself, but another part of her wanted him to stay. The same nonsensical part of her that wanted to wrap herself in his muscles and tell him all her secrets.

When they got to the entryway, Bastien stuck his hands in his pockets and shifted back on his heels. "A dozen moves on your own, huh?"

Before she could answer, before all the words she'd been holding inside could come tumbling out to the wrong person at the wrong time in the wrong place, his phone rang.

She snapped her mouth shut like she'd never opened it in the first place.

"I've got to take this—it's the electrician for the cabin." He had the door open in a flash, then looked over his shoulder one last time at her. "Let me know if you need anything, okay?"

She nodded, knowing she'd let the house come caving in on top of her before she'd ask for his help again.

Then he was gone.

FIVE
BASTIEN

Bastien drove away from Gabby with a lump in his throat the size of the mountains that surrounded Jasper Creek. It shouldn't be so hard to leave her. He barely knew her. This was just helping someone out who needed it, like he'd done hundreds of times before.

So why did he keep thinking about her hand tugging at her ponytail, and the way her lips had turned up in a smile when he'd told her the names of his fish?

Bastien pulled up in front of the cabin and headed inside, the lump doubling in size. When he walked across the shag carpet that might have once been white, now a sickening brownish gray, the lump slid down his chest to form a solid rock in his stomach. He took in the peeling paint, exposed wires, and smell of mold that permeated everything.

This morning, Nolan had said the cabin would need a lot of work. A more accurate description would be that it was a complete and total disaster, and Bastien was a complete idiot for thinking this was something he'd be able to do. On his own.

In less than three months.

While living in a tent in the backyard.

Bastien's feet crunched over the kitchen tile, and he closed his eyes, chest tight, praying he wouldn't see bones when he looked down. Two things kept him from turning around and walking out.

The first was what it would mean for Gabby to change his mind now. After seeing how little she'd brought with her, and hearing the hints of the rootless life she'd been living, he was more committed than ever to making sure she had a quiet, comfortable place to live while looking for her next room to rent. Though she hadn't been at Miller Family Medical long, he heard from people around town how great of a provider she was. Someone so smart and capable shouldn't have to do things on her own. Bastien was more than willing to help her, however he could.

The second was that if his parents really didn't want him to do this, then they would have just said no to the idea. Dr. James Miller III cared just as much about his family history as his son did, and he was simply too tired and too busy to do it himself. Bastien had learned how to give everything he had to his family from watching his dad.

His model for what a man, father, and husband should be was someone who put everyone else first. His dad had even let go of three generations of tradition without any fight to let his adored, Francophile wife give all their kids French names. Bastien did wonder sometimes how his life would have turned out as James Miller IV.

It was only since Anais had come home two years ago after finishing her residency that their dad had pulled back a little. Though only in his early sixties, retirement was on the horizon. Maybe he'd even finally take Bastien's mom to France like he'd been promising for years.

Then everything his dad did outside the clinic would fall on Bastien's shoulders.

The thought should have been comforting, but it didn't feel like enough.

The back door squeaked when Bastien opened it, and it

wobbled on its hinges, but it didn't fall off. Even if family history was important to his dad, home improvement had never been James Miller's forte. This project would be all Bastien's. His heart lifted. This was his way to contribute to the Miller family legacy in Jasper Creek.

Luckily, the sports camps he ran for the town wouldn't start for another week. This was the perfect time to get through the heavy demo stage of things. Sleeping in the tent wouldn't be the most comfortable, but it was temporary.

It would be an adventure. A break in the endless routine of school, coaching, family, and volunteering that left him in the same place every year while those around him moved on to the next phases of their lives. His dad's sacrifices had been for his wife and his children. Bastien's would be for his family and the town.

After grabbing a trash bag from his car, he made his way back into the kitchen to get started. The earlier crunches beneath his feet had been broken plates, not bones, and he uttered a soft prayer of thanks for that small bit of luck. Before he'd even filled the bag halfway, his phone rang.

It was Jackson. Disappointment washed over him, then he laughed at himself. There was no reason for Gabby to be calling him less than an hour after he'd left his house. Unless she couldn't find something or wasn't sure which cabinets she could use to put her stuff. He knew enough about her already to know she would rather figure it out on her own than ask him for anything.

Maybe that was why he hoped it was Gabby calling. Instead of him offering, he was hoping maybe she'd be asking for his help.

Yes, that's all he wanted. To help his ruinously beautiful new tenant. Nothing else.

He dropped the trash bag and swiped open his phone. "What's up, Jackson?"

"Are you already at the cabin?"

"Yeah, why?"

"What do you mean, why? We were supposed to go over together to meet Nolan."

"I called and you didn't pick up. I assumed you were... busy." He coughed. Most of the time he was thrilled his sister found happiness with his best friend.

Sometimes it made things unbelievably awkward.

"It was six in the morning. I was sleeping, now that I finally don't have hours of training."

"Sorry. I'm still on my school-year sleep schedule." He bent to pick up a few more loose pieces of wood and what might have been a set of mugs before someone smashed them. They made a loud clunk when he threw them into the bag.

"I'll be there as soon as I drop Anais off at your mom's for wedding stuff. Don't do everything without me."

"For once, I don't think I could even if I wanted to."

If there was one person Bastien didn't mind helping him, it was Jackson. His friend had been there for him a few years ago when Bastien had hurt himself right before the town's Halloween Festival, one of the most important fundraising events of the year for the town. Asking Jackson to do most of the heavy lifting for him hadn't been easy, but it had gone really well.

Not well enough that he wanted to admit to anyone else he needed help, of course.

Bastien would do as much as he could himself. Jackson should be there with Anais this morning. The cabin had a deadline, but that was way more flexible than changing a wedding date. So by the time Jackson showed up an hour later, Bastien had already moved on from the kitchen and into the living room.

"Whoa, I thought you said you wouldn't do everything without me." Jackson stepped around the pile of full trash bags that was nearly as tall as he was and slapped Bastien's shoulder in greeting.

"I have to finish this." Bastien looked up from what he was doing to see Jackson purse his lips in a familiar expression of disapproval. Holding up a hand to stop whatever lecture Jackson had planned, Bastien groaned. "You don't have to say it."

Jackson crossed his arms over his chest that—despite the lack of early-morning workouts—was still twice as large as Bastien's. "I reckon I do need to say it."

Everyone said he didn't have to do things on his own, but whether it was the town festivals or organizing extra training for the sports teams, people weren't exactly lining up to volunteer their own time. If he didn't do it, it wouldn't get done. Just like this cabin.

It may be all Bastien's project, but he was glad to have Jackson working alongside him.

"Can you help me with this?" Bastien lifted one end of a dilapidated couch, the only piece of furniture left in the entire house.

"You mean you can't do it by yourself?" Jackson raised an eyebrow but lifted the other end.

"Hey, I asked you to be here, didn't I?"

"You mean your sister volun-told me to be here to make sure you don't hurt yourself."

Bastien laughed at that, and the corner he was holding slipped a little.

"Got it?" The worry was evident in Jackson's voice.

"Fine." Bastien repositioned his hands and kept moving forward. "Not all of us have the muscles of a pro athlete."

There was only the smallest trace of bitterness in his voice. Six months into his retirement, Jackson still had the body of someone who'd been making his living through sports for over a decade. Meanwhile, Bastien did his best to fit in workouts around his busy schedule, so he hadn't been in that kind of shape since college.

Jackson knew him well enough to hear the whiff of Bastien's jealousy, but true friend that he was, he didn't say anything. They focused on getting the couch to the edge of the property. With simultaneous grunts, they heaved it down to the ground.

"Do you reckon you can get it done by the wedding?" Jackson

wiped his brow and looked up at the house. Though right now the facade was hard to see through the overgrown yard, it was typical for a cabin of the late 1800s in the area, with light wood siding and dark shutters.

Kicking away a fallen branch, Bastien ignored the gnawing pit in his stomach and nodded. "Nolan said it's just the roof... and the windows and floors. And the kitchen and bathroom. Replacing stuff that's rotted."

His friend let out a low whistle. "That sounds like a lot, Bash."

He waved that away. "It'll be fine. Hopefully there are some nice floors under that nasty carpet, and the electrician and plumber are coming next week. I'm not moving walls or doing anything fancy. Just getting it in good enough shape for a seller to not get too discouraged."

"Why do I feel like that means painting?"

Jackson groaned and Bastien chuckled. "Your favorite."

They'd spent one summer during college painting houses and the memories weren't the best.

"Well, there's no painting today at least." Jackson tugged at the cap on his head like he was staring down a pitcher with a wicked curveball. "You bring out the bags you've already filled, and I'll get started upstairs."

The rest of the day went by quickly, and the two men fell into their familiar pattern of work and casual chatter as they passed tools and equipment between them. It had been a while since Bastien had spent time with his friend, just the two of them, even though Jackson had moved permanently to Jasper Creek earlier that year. Of course, Bastien would have preferred to be at the Floodline drinking a beer together, rather than ripping out carpet nails and vacuuming dust bunnies six inches deep.

Around midafternoon, Jackson wiped his brow and looked at Bastien across the pile of old carpet they'd finally managed to remove from the stairs. "I'm worn slap out. About time for a beer?"

"Always. Want to ride over together?"

They waded through the grass in the front yard and passed the pile of trash bags that had accumulated to spectacular heights during the day. They were leaning unsteadily on the couch they'd brought out that morning. Bastien frowned and grabbed a few bags so that they wouldn't fall onto the road.

"Bash, what are you doing? The town has someone coming by tomorrow to get all that." Jackson was already beside Bastien's truck with the door halfway open.

"I know, I just want to move a few—" The pile tumbled onto the couch with a clatter, knocking it backward with an echoing thud. A leg broke off, and before Bastien could drop the trash bags, the couch crashed onto his foot. The crunch of bones was masked by the string of curses he let out.

Jackson turned, his eyes wide. "Bash, what happened?" He slammed the car door shut and ran over ten times faster than Bastien would have been able to if their positions had been reversed.

"My foot." Tears stinging his eyes, he managed to wrench himself out from under the couch. It was a strain on his muscles, already tired from the day's work, but he wasn't going to ask Jackson to lift it for him. His ankle was throbbing, along with all his toes. "Probably broken."

Jackson shook his head and wrapped his arm around Bastien's shoulder. "You'd know, wouldn't you? Why is it always your foot?"

With Jackson's support, Bastien hobbled to his truck. "Guess we're headed to the clinic instead of the Floodline," said Jackson.

Hot disappointment at missing out on more one-on-one time with his friend mixed with the vicious annoyance of knowing Anais would lecture him the second she saw him hobble into Miller Family Medical. Bastien groaned. "Just one drink first?"

As Jackson opened the car door, his lips turned up in a familiar sneaky smile Bastien hadn't seen in ages. "Only if you don't tell your sister."

SIX

GABBY

"Bastien Miller is in exam room three."

From her seat at the break room table, Gabby looked up from her tea and donut to see Hunter standing in the doorway, peering anxiously at her.

A thrill of anticipation snaked through Gabby's body that she quickly tamped down. *Bastien isn't here to see me. It's something medical.*

After spending an hour unpacking, she'd been called into work unexpectedly because Jane woke up with the flu. Gabby never said no to extra shifts, and the one Saturday they were open per month was usually pretty calm.

Dr. Austin Gibson appeared in the doorway next to Hunter. "What's he broken now?"

Gabby raised an eyebrow. "Does this happen a lot?"

Hunter and Austin both nodded, and Gabby added that little tidbit to what she knew about her friendly and accommodating landlord. Muscled and helpful. Eyes greener than cedar. Adorably obsessed with plants. Accident prone.

"Dr. Gibson's patient just arrived, so are you available to see Bastien?" Hunter asked.

"Of course." She smiled, and relief flashed across Hunter's face.

Despite her calm words, her heart had ticked up a notch at the thought of seeing him again so soon. She put aside her afternoon snack for later and washed her hands before following Hunter and Austin out into the hallway. When Hunter made his way back into the reception area, Austin cleared his throat right before she got to the exam room, and she turned to face him.

"Not today, but soon we should talk to Anais about scheduling." He kept his voice low, and Gabby frowned.

"Why?"

"She'll be busier than she realizes this summer, getting ready for the wedding." Austin shook his head. "There's no way this town is going to let her get away with some small, backyard thing."

"That makes sense." Their voices were quiet in the carpeted hallway. The walls were covered in drawings, holiday cards, and birth announcements, all proof of how much the town loved the Millers. Gabby was still getting excited comments from patients about Anais's news, even though it was almost a week old at this point.

"It'll mean more shifts for you, if you're okay with the overtime."

"Always." Gabby inhaled sharply, then ran a hand along her ponytail. "I mean, that's fine. Happy to help."

The doctor narrowed his eyes. "I know you have a long drive, so I don't want you to overdo it either."

Her eyes darted away, landing on one brightly colored drawing of a stick figure with the words "Thank you Dr. Anais" scribbled in crayon, before focusing on Austin again. "I moved... somewhere closer recently."

His face lit up with his brilliant flash of a smile. "I didn't know that. Great."

Gabby's heart gave a little happy tap against her chest. She liked Dr. Gibson. With his classic movie-star good looks, she'd overheard more than a few patients compare his intense blue eyes and dark hair to a certain red-caped superhero. While she wholeheartedly agreed with them, she'd never felt more for him than the genial cordiality she had for all colleagues.

That cordiality was what stopped her from admitting she was living in Jasper Creek. In Bastien's house. Bastien who was waiting for her to examine whatever injury he had. This was exactly why she didn't get deep into personal details with the people she worked with.

Well, not for this exact reason, but now she was glad for the distance.

"We'll chat more about the schedules next week. Have fun getting Bastien to listen to reason."

Warmth filled her chest when she realized she knew exactly what he meant. Though she could count their interactions on one hand, she already knew Bastien wasn't the type to back down easily if he thought he could help. Maybe he'd seen someone else moving in this afternoon and hurt himself while helping them. Taking a deep breath before opening the door, she slapped on the cheerful smile she used at work.

He's just another patient.

"How can I help you today, Bastien?"

With a single look at the bag of ice balanced on his shoeless foot and the pain etched on his face, Gabby was almost certain she knew what had happened. But she liked to hear everything the patient had to say before jumping to any conclusions. Maybe the foot was an unrelated flare-up of an old injury and he was actually here for stomach pains.

"I broke my toe. And sprained my ankle."

She pursed her lips to keep from smiling. Or maybe Gabby's first instinct had been right. "How did that happen?"

He groaned and hid his face behind his hands. "A couch fell on it."

Even though he couldn't see her, she raised an eyebrow. "Not buying me a new couch I hope?"

His hands fell away in an instant, and his eyes were wide and crinkled with worry. "Is something wrong with my couch?"

"Absolutely not." She bit back another smile. "Everything is fine. What happened?"

"I was at the Miller cabin I'm fixing up."

"Were you working there alone?" She bent to lift off the ice so she could examine the toe in question. "That's not safe."

He hissed in a breath when she gently touched the joint. "Jackson was there. He dropped me off, then went back to keep working. There's a lot to do."

There was a knock at the door, then Anais poked her head into the room. "I heard we had my favorite patient in here."

"Dr. Miller, I didn't know you were working today." Gabby frowned and looked at Bastien. "Are you okay with her coming in?"

He blinked at her, as if surprised that she would ask that. "Of course."

"Jackson texted me." Anais's eyes focused on his foot, and her expression turned sour. "Is it just me, or do you seem to hurt yourself way more than normal when you're with my fiancé?"

Bastien rolled his eyes. "You just wanted to bring him up so you could call him your fiancé, didn't you?"

Instantly, Anais brightened. She shot her brother a playful grin, and Gabby felt a prickle of jealousy. Their easy and playful interaction was proof of their picture-perfect sibling relationship. The kind Gabby had always wanted but would never have.

"So what's he done to himself now?"

Gabby raised her eyebrows at Bastien in question, and he sighed. "It's fine. It's not like Jackson won't tell her anyway. A couch fell on my foot."

The sharp inhale from Anais was both sympathetic and exasperated. "You really couldn't wait until after the wedding to hurt yourself?"

"It'll be fine by then." Bastien's tone was exponentially grouchier than it had been with Gabby. She was surprised he didn't stick his tongue out at his sister. "Broken toe is four weeks, max. Sprained ankle the same."

"And what about the cabin?"

Bastien's gaze flicked to Gabby's, then away just as quickly. "I'll figure it out." Worry fluttered in Gabby's stomach. Discreetly, she pressed a hand to it. She'd barely eaten that morning with the move, and she'd only eaten half of her donut, so it was a fifty-fifty chance this flutter would turn into something painful.

"You won't be able to drive," Anais said. "Jackson said you were planning on living there so you can work before and after the sports clinics. You can't do that if you're on crutches."

"I'll. Figure. It. Out." His jaw was clenched tight while Gabby's heart pounded in her chest.

The elation that had been coursing through her the past few days was quickly transforming into a familiar knot of anxiety deep in her gut.

A cheap, clean place to live less than two miles from work? Of course it was too good to be true.

Then, with a sudden drop of her heart, Gabby realized he hadn't told anyone she'd be living there. For a family that seemed to share everything, this seemed unusual, and she had to know why.

"I want to check Bastien for other injuries, if you don't mind stepping out for a moment, Dr. Miller?" Her tone was polite, her face smooth, revealing nothing of the turmoil inside of her.

"Of course." She shot Gabby a smile, then glared at her brother. "Stop by my office before you leave, Bastien."

Now Gabby had the urge to stick her tongue out at Anais as she walked out of the room.

That's not very professional. There was no reason for it other than the normal kind of protectiveness she'd have for any of her patients. That's all Bastien was right now. Not her landlord, who potentially would be telling her she had to move out less than twelve hours after she'd moved in. The tightness in her stomach was definitely turning into more, but she breathed through it as she smiled at Anais's retreating figure.

The second the door was closed, she turned to Bastien, ignoring the stabbing sensation in her belly. "I don't really need to check for other injuries if you don't want me to."

"I'm good, thanks." Bastien ran a hand through his hair and sighed miserably. "Sorry you had to see that."

His words tugged at her heart. Like having his sister fuss over him could ever be worse than what had happened with Gabby's. "It's fine. Families can be tricky."

Gabby took some medical tape from the cabinet to wrap his toe and fiddled with the end of it, struggling to open it. Right now, the focus was her patient, not her own spiraling anxiety.

Bastien leaned back on the exam table and chuckled, the picture of ease despite his swollen toes and ankle. "You sound like you're speaking from experience."

"Hmm." She concentrated on his toes so she wouldn't have to look him in the eyes.

"I'm not normally that crusty with her," he said.

With a snip of scissors, she finished up buddy-taping his big toe. "If you say so." She went back to the cabinet to get a wrap for his ankle.

"Fine, maybe I do get a little gruff, but only when she's being an insufferable know-it-all." When she looked over, he gave her a smirk. "Which is most of the time."

She grabbed the wrap, the corners of her lips turning up. If this had been coming from a coworker, she'd have ignored it. With Bastien, she could tell he was just venting. A perfectly normal thing for a patient to do.

"If you say so."

He stayed quiet as she wrapped his ankle, the heat of his skin searing through her latex gloves. The silence was heavy, the unspoken specter of the house floating in the air between them. What if he didn't bring it up? Would she have to ask him about it? Her breathing hitched, and she tucked in the ends of the bandage.

The second she was done, he pulled his leg away. "Don't worry, you can still live at my place." His words tumbled out in a rush, each one a sharp pinprick in the close, still air of the tiny exam room.

"I wasn't worried about that," she replied just as quickly. She stepped back from the table and nodded at his foot. "I'm worried about your toe."

Gabby was absolutely worried about the house. Even though the months she'd spent homeless as a child were long in the past, where she'd be sleeping at night would always be on her mind until she had a place of her own.

"I can still live at the Miller cabin with crutches." He gestured at his foot. "I literally have crutches more often than I don't. I'm very nimble with them. They're easier for me than a boot, in case you were about to suggest one."

She was shaking her head before he'd even finished talking. "Bastien, you know you can't live at the cabin. It's fine. I'll find something else."

She could practically see his mind whirring away, trying to figure out how to help her.

"What else have you broken?" she asked in an attempt to distract him from trying to solve a problem that wasn't his to worry about. She leaned against the wall, arms crossed, ready to listen.

"Oh, everything." He ticked all his various injuries off on his fingers, then started over when he got to ten.

It wasn't funny, but the way he tallied everything like he was going for a world record made her chuckle. She shook her head when he'd finally finished the never-ending list. "I'm surprised you didn't fix up your foot yourself if you're such an expert at breaking things."

"I probably could." He rubbed the stubble on his chin and

shrugged. "But why not take advantage of having all these doctors in the family?"

It was supposed to be a joke, but she sensed something else, something painful, hidden in his words, and in the easy way he leaned on the table. All she managed was a small smile, and his own wide grin faded. There was another beat of silence.

"What if..." He bit his lip, looked away, then back at her, his eyes greener than ever. "What if we lived there together?"

Her stomach dipped. Pushing off the wall, she sucked in a breath. It was the simplest and most logical solution, of course. But it was also the most complicated, for so many reasons. The biggest being her uncontrollable urge to tell him everything about herself. So far, she'd resisted, but if they were living together, she knew she wouldn't even last a week.

"I won't be there much." He nodded at his foot. "Even with this, I still have the camps to run, and I'll be at the cabin as many hours a day as possible."

That was a good point.

Her hand reached up to her ponytail, and she slid her fingers through its smooth strands, her heartbeat jumping. "Why didn't you tell your family I was renting it?"

"What do you mean?"

"Anais didn't say anything about it just now."

He scratched at the scar just above his right eye that she now knew was from getting accidentally hit in the head with a baseball by Jackson in college. "I don't really think it's their business where you live unless you want to tell them."

Warm gratitude rushed through her chest. "So will you tell them if we're living there together?"

That was something very different, and much more likely to complicate her working situation.

"No." His eyes were glued to hers and full of such a generous glow, Gabby could barely breathe. "It's up to you."

At the familiar words, her heart raced. The memory of their

first interaction came rushing to the front of her mind. Not that it was ever far. Every time she got into her car, she thought of him.

"You said the same thing at your parents' Easter picnic." She gathered up the tape and scissors and busied herself with putting them away. "When you helped me with my car, and I asked you if you'd tell anyone about it."

The Easter picnic at the Millers' had been a lovely afternoon, even if Gabby had mostly stayed on the periphery of things. There were Austin and Hunter and Jane and the Miller family, all seven of them, but there were also people from the town. Carl from the café with his dad and daughter, Tina from the bookstore with her wife. People Gabby knew by sight but hadn't talked to much in the handful of weeks between her starting work and the party.

Rather than get to know any of them, however, she'd left early, overwhelmed by how close and happy they all seemed. Like they didn't have any care in the world, like life was perfect.

Then she'd gotten into her car and it wouldn't start, and Bastien had swooped in like a knight in shining armor and khaki shorts.

Bastien shrugged, like he'd shrugged then, like it was no big deal. Like she was allowed to keep her secrets and he wouldn't judge her for not wanting to tell everyone about her life the way everyone in Jasper Creek seemed to.

"It's your life, Gabby. I just want to help you live it however you want."

With anyone else, she wouldn't have believed it. But when Bastien said it, something in her trusted it completely, in a way she never had with anyone else.

Maybe because no one had ever helped her the way he'd managed to do not just once, but now twice.

"Alright then. We'll both live at the house."

SEVEN

BASTIEN

There was a woman sleeping in his house for the first time in five years, and Bastien didn't know what to do. He watched the gray predawn light trickle in across his ceiling and counted to one hundred, hoping an idea would come to him.

He spent Saturday night and all of Sunday at his parents' house, claiming he wanted to give them their own chance to fuss over his injury. Really, it was to give Gabby at least one full day in the house alone.

Now he was back in his own bed, wondering what else he could do for her, and coming up empty. All his early-morning brain wanted to supply him with were painful memories that pushed him down further into bed with a heaviness that had nothing to do with his weighted blanket.

Brenda had never stayed over that much. It was like she only enjoyed the public side of their relationship, being seen with him around town, going out to dinner, holding his arm at town events and smiling at people. The private part of the relationship—dealing with the day-to-day of how to make a life together when he was a teacher with a six a.m. wake up time and a coach whose evenings and weekends were full of sports practices and games—wasn't something Brenda had been interested in.

Gabby isn't Brenda.

He turned onto his side, and his brand-new digital alarm clock blinked from 5:59 to 6:00.

First of all, she's not my girlfriend.

It was the truth, but not one he was happy with. The craving for something more with the shy yet forceful blond nurse had been there since he'd helped her with her car at his parents' party months ago. It was that kind of instant attraction that overwhelms you, grabbing hold of you and dragging you down before you even know what's happening.

She'd been so grateful when he restarted her car, looking at him like he'd saved her life. It felt too much like taking advantage of her in a bad situation to ask her out then, even if every brain cell had been begging him to.

He could have asked her out any time after that, however, and he should have. Then maybe he wouldn't be in this situation, tossing and turning in his bed, wondering how to make sure she felt welcome without it being weird.

The lamp and clock had clearly been the wrong move. She was paying him to live here—it wasn't like she was here on vacation. Now that they were roommates, did that mean he should do more? Or less?

The clock blinked again. 6:15.

Should he make breakfast? Leave out the cereal and milk for her to serve herself? They'd talked about how to split living expenses, and Gabby had insisted on paying for all of her own groceries. One of the few boxes she'd brought with her contained her dishes and kitchenware, which she assured him she'd wash herself. Basically, she'd made it perfectly clear this was a co-living situation, not a typical roommate situation.

Sounds familiar.

Bastien pulled the blanket over his head.

Gabby wasn't Brenda, but the ache in his chest at the thought of how separate she wanted to keep things was too familiar to ignore. Brenda had kept very few things at Bastien's place, never talked about moving out of her apartment, lived an entirely separate life from him in all the ways that mattered.

It should have raised red flags much earlier, of course, but Bastien wasn't that happy with his life either at the time. He was so busy being frustrated at not being a professional soccer player that he didn't realize until much later that Brenda was upset about the same thing.

By then, she'd moved on to someone more important. Someone who could give her everything she needed.

That's not what this is. Gabby's just a roommate.

The clock made a little beep to let him know it was six thirty, and his hand shot out from under the blanket to turn it off. With a sigh, he sat up and rubbed his face, knowing it was pointless to try to sleep more.

Getting to his feet, his chest tightened to know Anais would never find herself in this situation. His twin always had a plan, always had the next few steps mapped out. Jackson had been the biggest interruption to her ordered life, but not really. She'd always wanted to get married, have kids, work with their dad at the clinic. If she married a former baseball player instead of a doctor like she'd planned, that wasn't really a big change. Jackson was still the steady, supportive kind of man like their dad, and it was no big surprise that's who Anais ended up with.

Living with Gabby was definitely not Bastien's plan. Yet here he was, in over his head like always, thanks to his overly generous nature. Somehow he'd figure it out, like he always did. By shoving down his own feelings and needs to avoid being a bother to anyone.

Dread heavy in his chest, he dragged himself downstairs, careful as he hopped on one foot to skip the creaky stair so he wouldn't wake Gabby up. When she'd helped him bring in his stuff from his car the previous day, she'd wanted him to have the downstairs guest room because of his foot. But there was nothing new for him about going up and down stairs when injured. Besides, all her stuff was already unpacked down there, and she'd balked at his offer to help her pack it up again.

In the end, her desire for privacy and independence won, and Bastien suspected it always would with her.

By the time he got to the kitchen, it was nearly seven. He went into autopilot, making coffee and eggs like he did every morning. The presence of the crutches he'd grabbed from their place at the bottom of the stairs didn't even change his routine that much. It wasn't the first or even the tenth time he'd had to make his way around the kitchen doing things one-handed.

He stopped himself from making more eggs, but he did make enough coffee for two people. That seemed like a good compromise if she didn't want to split cooking duties or costs. Who could say no to coffee?

Half an hour later, Gabby came out of her room and walked into the kitchen, already dressed in her scrubs for the clinic. There was the briefest falter in her step when she saw Bastien leaning against the counter, but she quickly smoothed a smile across her face that didn't quite hide the pink tinge in her cheeks.

"Good morning."

Hot awareness of her half-averted gaze prickled across his skin, and he realized with a drop of his stomach he was still in his boxers and t-shirt. Autopilot apparently did not involve getting dressed when it had been only him in this house for so long. There was only one option to avoid eternal embarrassment and awkwardness: pretend like he'd just rolled out of bed even though he'd been up for an hour pondering the breakfast question.

"Morning." He yawned, then sipped from his mug in what he hoped was a sleepy way. "I made coffee."

"Thanks, I'll be fine." She held up an electric kettle in her hand that he hadn't noticed before. "Is it okay if I plug this in?"

"Yes." He set his mug on the counter and reached for it. She pulled back slightly, and he let out a frustrated sigh. "Gabby, I'm okay with not sharing food, but we are sharing the space. We'll be touching each other's stuff."

She inhaled sharply and let out a little chuckle. "I know. I'm sorry. I haven't had caffeine yet."

"You like tea rather than coffee?" He tucked away that piece of information. Despite having just finished breakfast, his stomach ached, hungry for information about her.

She nodded and stepped forward with her kettle at the same time he moved to take it. Her arm brushed against his, sending a trembling energy shooting through his body. Her eyes were wide, just on the edge of sleepy, her lips a deep berry pink. Everything about her was pulling him toward her.

Bastien stepped back and slid his hand through his hair, taking one last inhale of the irresistible smell of roses that had somehow flooded the kitchen. "I'll get out of your way."

Before Gabby could respond, he grabbed his crutches and rushed from the room, thankful now that the years of practice with them meant he could move so quickly.

This was going to be harder than he thought.

———

GABBY

As Gabby watched Bastien clomp away—quite gracefully really—on his crutches, she felt the familiar sharp stab of anxiety deep in her gut.

This wasn't going to be as easy as she'd hoped.

It should have been. After all, she'd lived with countless roommates over the years, all genders, all personalities, all orientations.

She set down her kettle on the spotless counter, plugged it in, then put her mug next to it. The familiar ritual should have calmed her, the tidiness of the house should have reassured her, and yet her hand shook as she opened the packet of tea and placed it in her mug.

She'd lived with people who left their clothes and trash everywhere, people who had parties all night while Gabby was trying to study, people who fled in the middle of the night but left all their stuff for her to deal with. When the room was cheap, she didn't ask too many questions, and she'd learned to put up with any situation.

The kettle whistled and she poured the hot water into her mug, the steam warming her already flaming cheeks. Living with Bastien was going to be a completely new experience. The attraction she thought was one-sided might not be, and that had never been something she'd dealt with before. All of her most handsome and rugged roommates, guys who put even Austin to shame, had been easy to slot into the friend/roommate category.

It was like Gabby could shut off that part of her entirely when there was a goal to focus on. Whether it was finishing nursing school, getting her master's degree, or putting everything she could into her job, there was always something more important to keep her from getting involved with a roommate and bringing unnecessary drama into her life.

"Drama is too expensive," she whispered to herself, then inhaled the dark, nutty warmth of English Breakfast tea.

It wasn't quite enough to erase Bastien's fresh, early-morning spiciness still lingering in the kitchen. She knew nothing would ever erase the image of him in boxers and rumpled bed-head hair. It was burned into her brain forever.

Luckily they had a lease, something she'd insisted on now that they'd both be living there. She didn't want there to be any issues if people at work found out where she was living for the summer. The lease clearly laid out what each party was responsible for in terms of meals and cleaning. These were her standard roommate boundaries, and should keep her crush-like feelings under control. Or at least well hidden. She had her own dishes and food, and she'd do her fair share of the general cleaning. It wouldn't be hard to time things for when he wasn't at the house, since he had both the cabin and sports camps to manage all summer.

She finished up her tea and unplugged her kettle. After quickly washing her mug, she took everything back to her bedroom. On her way through the living room to the other side of the house, she noticed again how clean everything was. Much cleaner than she'd expected.

So he knows how to use a vacuum. Big deal. Still not worth the drama of getting involved with him.

Back in her room, she realized she had almost a full hour until she had to leave for work now that it was only a short walk. It had been ages since she'd had this kind of free time in the morning. In the past, she'd have classes to study for or tutoring to prep. She was at a loss for what to do.

Her stomach rumbled, and as she rubbed it, an idea popped into her head. Maybe instead of the cereal bars she had in her room, she could have breakfast at Carl's Café. There was an enthusiastic leap in her gut. It was a small indulgence, one she didn't make often, but with savings from gas and the cheapest rent she'd had in over a year, ten dollars wouldn't totally blow her budget.

Just as she grabbed her purse and reached for the door, that nasty little inner voice spoke up.

Are you sure?

The instinct to save every single penny was a hard one to ignore. Gabby hesitated with her hand over the door handle, her pulse racing. Ten dollars wasn't going to make the difference between owning and not owning a house—she knew that rationally.

Her heart that had been battered and bruised by years of lack, however, wasn't quite ready to let all of those fears go.

With a sigh, she dropped her hand, put her purse back on the chair, grabbed a cereal bar, and sat down at the desk to take another look at her budget. When these kinds of thoughts popped up, the only thing that seemed to help was going through the numbers again. And again. And again.

No amount of reassurance ever seemed enough, and maybe never would be. Gabby hadn't just been poor growing up, she'd been homeless more than once, her mom barely able to take care of herself, let alone two little girls.

She'd learned to rely on herself, and only herself. As nice as people could be, they weren't the ones who'd have to deal with the consequences of her mom's actions. They weren't the ones who could keep her from repeating the same mistakes as her mom. Gabby was.

So she'd studied and planned. In family shelters, on couches in the apartment of a random "friend" of her mom's, and even a few cold nights in the back seat of a car.

That wasn't her life anymore, and she was determined it never would be again. The years of sacrifice and single-mindedness had paid off. Now she saved and planned and saved some more, in tiny rooms rented in cash with her pile of boxes always ready to go. She kept track of every penny and felt a wild thrill of pride each time she reached a milestone she never thought she would. Paying off her student loans. Buying her car. And soon, buying a house.

"Gabby?" The deep, intimate timber of Bastien's voice sent a shiver down her spine. He knocked softly. "Just wanted to let you know I'm leaving. Jackson's here to pick me up."

"Okay." Her heart did a little cartwheel in her chest. He wasn't going to tell her every time he left, was he?

She liked the thought of that way too much.

"I'll be back around six."

A smile spread across her lips. Yes, he was going to be like this, and she didn't mind one bit.

"Okay, thanks."

She heard him shuffle around on his crutches in front of her door, like maybe he wanted to knock again or say more, but there was a faint honk and he thumped away.

There'd be time to think about him later. Once she had a house, a stable foundation to build a life, the security she'd been craving that could only come from her own hard work. She was so close to getting everything she wanted, she couldn't start to rely on someone else. No matter how sweet and thoughtful he might be.

EIGHT
BASTIEN

Bastien had spent hours in locker rooms, in buses full of sweaty athletes after away games, and in cramped off-campus housing. He could say with complete confidence that he'd never smelled worse than after working all day in a house that hadn't been lived in for over four decades.

Jackson apparently agreed.

"You need a shower." His friend was driving him home after they finished what they could for the day, which hadn't been much considering Bastien was on crutches.

He mostly sanded, which he could do sitting down, but even with the windows open, the day was humid, and the cabin wasn't well ventilated. Surprising, considering its history as a tuberculosis clinic, but patients mostly stayed outside on the wide porch, in bunks that hadn't left much room between them.

Didn't it kind of defeat the purpose of sleeping outside, he wondered, if you were still breathing in the air of the people next to you? For all he knew, it did help. After all, he wasn't the doctor in the family.

"Can I take it at your place?"

Jackson glanced his way with a raised eyebrow before making

the turn that would get them back into town. "Is your shower broken?"

"No." Bastien shifted in his seat, hissing in pain when he banged his toe against the door. "I have a roommate for the summer."

Now Jackson's head turned completely toward him, his mouth set in a familiar hard line of disapproval. Luckily, they were at a stop sign, or they'd probably have run off the road.

"Bash, please tell me it's a dog and not some charity case you decided to take in on top of the house and camps and—"

"It's not a charity case." He scratched his chin. The stubble there was full of sawdust and itched like crazy. "It's Gabby. Her roommate gave her like, two days to move out last week."

"Oh." Jackson frowned, pondering this for so long, someone honked behind them. He moved forward slowly, his eyes fixed on the road while worrying his bottom lip with his teeth.

"Don't tell Anais please." It was a pointless request, but Bastien had to try. "It's Gabby's business where she lives, so it shouldn't matter at work."

"It shouldn't matter that she's living with her boss's son?"

"Living with me makes it sound like we're dating. Which we're not." Hiding in her room that morning had sent a pretty clear sign she was not interested in anything like that. "Technically I'm her landlord."

"You have a lease?"

"Yes. We didn't at first when I was going to live at the cabin all summer. But then with my toe, I had to move back in, and it seemed better to have something in writing."

He'd been fine without one, but Gabby had insisted, and he wasn't about to say no to anything she asked. Not when it was his own stupid fault she wouldn't have what he'd promised her.

"Well, at least you haven't totally lost all reason."

He might have though. Less than twenty-four hours living in the same house and she'd been on his mind all day.

"Anais will ask why you're showering at our place."

"I'll tell her my shower is broken so you don't have to be the one to lie to her." Unlike Jackson, he relished any opportunity to hide the truth from Anais, since it happened so rarely. His life would be much easier the less she knew about him. "She'll be so happy to be able to fuss over my toe and scold me again that she won't question it."

The corner of Jackson's lips twitched.

"Fine, but this can't go on all summer."

Bastien held up his hands. "It's not up to me."

Jackson rolled his eyes and turned left instead of right at the next street.

When they got to Anais and Jackson's house, however, Anais wasn't there. Bastien showered quickly, cleaning up as best he could, but knowing perfectly well his sister's eagle eyes would know he'd been there somehow. The bottles of shampoo and soap would both be a centimeter lower than they were this morning or whatever.

At least he didn't smell like he'd been rolling around in mold and mud all day anymore. Anticipation heated his veins as Jackson drove him home. Gabby said she'd take care of her own meals, but they could at least sit together at the kitchen table, couldn't they? Bastien was looking forward to it more than he wanted to admit.

Declining Jackson's offer to help him to the door, Bastien waved goodbye to his friend and eagerly lurched up the front path on his crutches. With a shaking hand, he opened the door and walked into...

An empty house.

"Hello?" He shuffled around, making as much noise as possible in case Gabby was wearing headphones in her room or something. After a slow hobble through the downstairs, he made his way to her door and knocked.

Nothing. She wasn't there.

Unease roiled in his gut. It was past seven, later than he'd told her he'd be home. He hadn't even thought to ask her about her hours. The clinic closed at five thirty, though his dad and Anais usually stayed until six to finish up paperwork. Maybe there was extra paperwork an NP had to handle too.

A quick glance out the window confirmed she'd walked today instead of taking her ancient car. The first threads of panic began to weave themselves around his chest. The clinic wasn't far, but there were a few roads without sidewalks. If something had happened to her when he could have offered to drive her this morning, he'd never forgive himself.

Stop overreacting.

This could be her routine. Maybe she went to the Floodline after work or to Carl's Café for dinner. Even if she was his roommate and tenant, she was first and foremost an adult with a life who could keep whatever hours she wanted.

None of these very logical thoughts kept the worry from eating away at his chest like rust had consumed the old appliances in the cabin. When the door finally opened a half hour later, he practically jumped from his seat on the couch.

"You're okay."

Gabby stopped halfway through the door, blinked a few times, then a little crease appeared between her eyebrows. "Yes. Why wouldn't I be?" Her dark eyes flashed with an emotion he couldn't quite decipher.

"It's just, um, later than I thought you'd be home?" He cringed, instantly hearing how weird it was to say that. "Not that you need to be home at a specific time. Or need to tell me when you'll be home."

Now she was looking at him like his dad did when he was trying to figure out what kind of terminal illness Bastien had when all he'd done was cough once. All the worry that had been building over the past hour was now a lump of embarrassment stuck thick in his throat.

He rubbed his hands along his face and took a deep breath.

"Sorry. I haven't had a roommate in a long time, and I've never been a landlord. Can we start over?" He gave her a small, apologetic smile, hoping it held enough to make her understand that he wasn't feeling anything other than friendly concern. "Go back out and come back in?"

The corners of her lips twitched. "Really?"

He nodded, encouraged by the fact she hadn't just stormed off to her room and slammed the door. Or worse, ignored him completely and not spoken a word all evening. Both of which had been the favorite responses of Brenda's whenever he was being too needy. "Let's have a do-over. I can be a totally awesome roommate-slash-landlord, I promise."

Now a smile was spreading slowly over her face, transforming it from exhausted and wary to a kind of simmering mischief that made his heart beat so hard it might burst from his chest.

Without another word, she turned around and went out the door. His blood pounded in his ears as he waited for her to come back in, and he quickly spread his body over the couch, arranging it in a relaxed, lounging posture that kept his toes and wrapped ankle away from anything hard he might accidentally hit. He took out his phone and opened a random sports scores site, scrolling away while he waited for her to come back.

The door creaked open, and Gabby walked into the living room.

"Oh, hey," he said and looked up briefly from his phone with a quick smile. "How was your day?"

"Fine." He could hear the smile in her voice, and it was a struggle to not look up and take in its full glory. There'd be time for that in the days and weeks to come. "Anais, Austin, and I were going over the schedules for the summer."

"Changes to the schedule? You sure Anais was there?"

Her throaty chuckle had his toes curling. He glanced up to see her tugging her hair out from the tight ponytail it was always in.

She ran a hand through it, shaking out the long golden strands, and his mouth went dry.

"Austin was able to convince her. We'll stay open three nights per week until seven instead of one Saturday a month. Gives everybody more time on the weekends."

"That sounds like a great idea."

"Thanks. How was your day?"

"Good." Feigning a nonchalance she'd know was a lie if she could hear the frantic patter of his heart in his chest, he yawned and scratched his chin, still itchy even after the shower, then looked back down at his phone. "I sanded eight thousand planks of wood and didn't break anything else."

"Well, that does sound like a good day."

There was a heavy hint of teasing in her words, and his chest swelled with a burning, tentative hope. Her bag hit the floor with a clunk, followed by a soft clop when her shoes fell to the floor. He glanced up again and she had them in her hands.

"You can leave your stuff by the door."

"It's okay. I don't want things to get too cluttered." She shrugged and looked away. Like cold water on a hot pan, hope sizzled away in a single heartbeat and a desperate, jittery kind of energy took its place. His phone dropped to his lap. He knew he would say the wrong thing, but he had to try something.

"You're probably hungry. Even if we're each doing our own thing for food, I don't mind eating together at the table if you want some company."

"Maybe another night. Austin and I grabbed something after Anais went home."

A heaviness settled in his body, and it took him a few breaths before he could speak. "Okay, cool."

Even to his ears, he sounded angry and jealous. The opposite of an awesome roommate-slash-landlord.

This time it was easy to keep his eyes on his phone, avoiding her gaze that he could feel burning into the side of his head. A few uncomfortable moments passed.

"Have a good night, Bastien."

"Sure."

The sadness in her words broke his heart in two. He nodded once and raised a hand as a parting gesture, his gaze still glued to his phone. The gentle click of her bedroom door closing was like a punch to the chest.

NINE
GABBY

"How well do you know Bastien?" Gabby asked Austin the next day at work.

Austin looked up from his phone. "Pretty well, why?"

He was leaning against the counter in the break room, resplendent in his lustrous, raven-haired glory. The only thing marring his perfect face was the frown that pulled down his lips and made a furrow between his brows. Even with that, he was, by anyone's standards, blazingly handsome.

Gabby's heart wasn't pattering away because of that, however. In her mind, she was picturing green eyes locked on a phone and a long, lean body spread across a couch that had gone from relaxed to rigid in just a few moments.

"It's nothing. I just hear a lot of patients mention him." Not a lie, but it was the older Mrs. Fosters of the town who talked about how helpful he was, or the moms discussing how well he coached their kids. "He doesn't seem like the type to date around, but does he?"

Austin's gaze was hard to read, and Gabby was careful to keep her expression blandly attentive like she would when listening to a patient describe their symptoms. Her hands gripped her mug, and she tried to calm her racing pulse as she leaned back in her chair in what she hoped was a nonchalant way.

"I don't think he's been with anyone since Brenda."

Gabby nodded and took a sip of her tea as if this was only mildly interesting and not like she had eight thousand follow-up questions.

This morning, she'd heard a honk outside just before seven, so she knew her roommate-slash-landlord wouldn't be waiting for her with coffee in the kitchen again... in his boxers. She definitely wasn't upset about that. Having the house to herself had been the original plan, and she was grateful for the space and privacy.

But she was curious about his sudden shift in mood the night before. She couldn't ask Anais, obviously. Austin was about the same age as the Miller twins and had been working in Jasper Creek for over a year and a half. He'd been at the Easter picnic and knew the family well. He would know something about Bastien.

"And Brenda was how long ago?" Over the rim of her mug, she cast Austin a quick glance.

"About five years or so." Austin tucked his phone into his pocket and crossed his arms. "Can I ask you something without you getting mad?"

Well, that question never leads to anything good.

Heart racing, she forced herself to laugh. It came out in an awkward puff of air. "That sounds like you already know it'll make me mad."

"After paying for dinner last night, I get one free pass."

Of course there was a catch to his kindness yesterday. There was always a catch. Her throat tightened, and she frowned down at her tea. "That's not what I meant when I said I'd pay you back."

They'd eaten tacos in the park and discussed an article they'd both read about treating patients with alcohol use disorder. It was so perfectly mundane, she wasn't sure Austin even realized the milestone it had been for her. She never went out to eat with colleagues. Or let them pay for her. But Austin was, if nothing else, very charming. It had nothing to do with his looks and more to do with the intelligent and vaguely piratical glint his eyes got when he was clearly thinking five steps ahead of the conversation.

"Are you dating Bastien Miller?"

Gabby let out a strangled cough. "What?" Tacos had clearly been a mistake. This was exactly why she kept up barriers. "I thought you wanted to ask which patients talk about you."

Austin fixed his intense blue gaze at her, eyebrows raised, waiting for an answer.

"I'm not *dating* him." She slid her hand over her ponytail, sleek and tight like it always was. "I'm renting his spare room for the summer."

"Well, that explains why I saw you walking down his street last night." Austin shifted his position on the counter, his face aglow with amusement.

"Why were you on his street?"

"I was visiting someone."

"Who?" Gabby's eyes widened. "I'm sorry, that's none of my business."

"I just asked you about yours." His lips turned up. "You're allowed to know personal things about your colleagues, you know."

Now Gabby's face heated, and she knew it was also turning a bright pink. So he'd noticed she kept the conversation entirely professional the night before.

"I know. I just like my privacy."

"We'll be working together a lot this summer, so I'm sure we'll learn more about each other."

The air in the break room was getting stuffy. "Like what?"

"Like..." Austin tilted his head back and forth. "Are you originally from Colorado?"

This wasn't what she thought he'd want to know. It couldn't hurt to tell him, could it? With a quick glance over her shoulder at the door, she checked no one else was walking by.

"No, I grew up in California."

"So did I." His tone was conversational, but his eyes glinted in the fluorescent overhead lights of the break room. Somehow, he'd already known that about her. "See, that wasn't so hard, was it?"

The knot in her chest was as tight as ever, but Gabby couldn't help but smile as she scooted back from the table, her chair scraping the floor. Despite all her carefully constructed walls and boundaries, someone peeking through wasn't as terrible as she thought it would be. "Well, now you know where I grew up and where I'm living this summer. Anything else?"

"For now, that's plenty." Austin flashed her a grin, all teeth and charm. "Feel free to ask me anything about your new landlord that you want."

She pursed her lips and stood up, empty mug in hand. "I'll be fine, thanks." It only took her a minute to rinse out her mug and put it away while Austin grinned at her like he'd won the lottery.

"You never answered my question." She put her hand on her hip and turned to face him. "Who were you visiting last night?"

The grin disappeared in an instant. "Nobody important."

If two words had ever held more stinging regret, Gabby had never heard them. Austin's beautiful face was transformed into something full of an aching sadness, but only for a moment. As if she'd imagined it, he was all joviality again. With a cocky tilt to his eyebrow, he leaned on one arm on the counter.

"If it were something worth sharing, you'd all know about it. Don't worry."

Gabby let her eyes linger on his open, yet somehow still guarded, expression. It was the same one she'd learned to master over the years, the one that kept everyone at a distance—except for Austin apparently. His unique combination of charm, intelligence, and genuine interest had gotten more out of her in ten minutes than she ever intended to share.

She could see herself trusting him, but did he trust her?

Her lips twisted into a furtive smile. "We'll be working

together a lot this summer, so I'm sure we'll learn more about each other."

Austin barked out a laugh and stood up, shaking his head. "I guess we will."

With her chest full of a new kind of warmth, Gabby left him in the break room to get ready for her next patient. It wasn't the kind of giddiness she felt around Bastien, but a smoother, steadier glow that hinted at more nights eating tacos and talking about journal articles. Or maybe even more personal topics.

Making friends wasn't something she did easily, but she already knew it would be impossible for the summer to end without Austin becoming one of hers.

There was no time to work on her friendship with Austin that week, however, thanks to a bout of summer flu making its way through the community. There was barely time to eat at work, let alone spend the time on the kind of small talk Gabby usually avoided.

As exhausted as she was after every stressful day of work, she didn't go right home. She forced herself to walk around Jasper Creek, exploring the town in the sunny evenings, avoiding the inevitable awkward interactions with Bastien at home. It was like the air escaped from her lungs any time she was near him, making it impossible to form words. She knew he must think she was weird or snobby. All her other roommates had. It was easier to let them—and him—assume that than to risk getting closer and letting something slip.

Friday after work, she discovered the library in Jasper Creek was within walking distance of both the clinic and Bastien's house. With a giddy sense of joy, she filled her bags with enough books and movies to last her all month, smiling when she stumbled on some favorites that she hadn't found at other, larger libraries.

Apparently, people in Jasper Creek were fans of science fiction comedy like she was.

Then, on the way home, she'd gotten a call from the tutoring service she worked for. They had a few students looking for some help this summer. The next five Sundays were booked solid for her, and the shimmering promise of owning her own home was growing brighter and brighter.

Now it was Saturday and she had an entire day to do whatever she wanted for the first time in months. If Bastien was following his usual schedule, he'd already left and wouldn't be back until after she'd closed herself into her room for the night. The house was empty of his distracting and confusing presence.

She was just settling onto the couch when she heard someone moving around upstairs.

"Bastien?" Her voice shook.

"Gabby?" There was the slow creak of the stairs, and he appeared in the living room a minute later with a single crutch under one arm and the bleary eyes of someone who'd just woken up.

"I thought you were at the cabin." Her voice was calm, but her heart was racing. Did he want the living room to himself? Should she go back into her room?

"Jackson had to do wedding stuff with Anais, and I'm not allowed to drive yet." He yawned, stretching his arms high to reveal a line of tight ab muscles where his t-shirt rode up. Like a magnet, her eyes were drawn directly to it, and her already racing heart sped up to a highly unhealthy pace.

He dropped his arms and his gaze settled on her. There was a prickle of awareness when his eyes landed on the large rose tattoo on her shoulder. Shivers raced up and down her arms at the way his eyes traced the dark edges of it, taking in the bright, contrasting colors she'd spent hundreds of dollars she couldn't afford to get just right. Pulling her eyes away from his shirt, she reached for the blanket she'd brought from her room and wrapped it around her shoulders.

A slight upward tilt of his eyebrows told her he wanted to ask about the tattoo. Her muscles tightened underneath the blanket, her favorite fluffy pink one she'd taken from house to house through countless moves.

This was why she never wore sleeveless shirts unless she was at home alone. Why she was always dressed by the time she went into the kitchen in the morning.

"Anyway, I kind of needed the rest." He took a step toward the couch. "It's been a long week."

The pace of her pulse slowed to something resembling a typical rhythm.

"Same here." She inhaled deeply, knowing there was only one thing to do, what any normal roommate would offer. Something she'd never done or offered before. "I was going to watch a movie, if you want to join me?"

"Really?" His eyes lit up, and Gabby's heart leaped in a very un-roommate-like way. Then his shoulders curved forward and he cleared his throat. "It's okay. I can see you were looking forward to a day on your own. I can call Eli or Dani to go out somewhere."

Everything in her chest softened. Even in his own house, completely exhausted, he was putting her needs first. This, more than anything else, made her turn fully toward him with what she hoped was an inviting expression.

"Those are your two youngest siblings? I don't think I met them at the picnic last month." Not that she'd talked to many people before she'd run off to her broken car.

Bastien nodded and took a few uneven steps toward the couch, but didn't sit down. "They only just got home from college for the summer. Elias finished his freshman year in pre-med, and Danielle's going to start med school in the fall."

"Everyone in your family really is a doctor." She'd heard it, but it hadn't really clicked until now. Miller Family Medical wasn't just the name of the clinic but a brand. "You're the odd one out."

She meant it as a compliment, but he pursed his lips, shifting his weight back and forth on his single crutch.

"What about you?" he asked before she could give in to the urge to share how she was the odd one out in her family for even having a job. "Any siblings?"

"No." It was a lie, but one she'd told so often it slid right off her tongue. There was only the smallest prickle of guilt deep in the innermost part of her chest. She pushed it aside like she always did and tucked the blanket tighter around her, making sure the tattoo was entirely covered.

He flopped down onto the easy chair opposite the couch and lifted his injured foot onto the coffee table.

"What should we watch?" Without looking at her, he raked his hand through his hair.

It was rumpled from sleep, and Gabby ached to smooth her fingers over his wayward brown strands, putting it back in order, taking care of him in some small way to make up for all the things he'd done for her so far.

"What are you in the mood for?" There were some of her favorite movies in the pile, and Gabby told herself she wouldn't be upset if he didn't like any of them, but her heart pounded away as he sifted through the stack.

"Anything." He held up one. "You seem to like sci-fi and fantasy."

Her breath hitched. "We don't have to watch those. There are regular movies too."

He turned to raise an eyebrow at her. "That wasn't a criticism, Gabby. Just a comment."

Of course it was. What was wrong with her? She scrunched up her face. "Sorry. I'm not really used to talking to my roommates."

His lips pursed into a thin line. "Well, considering the most recent one kicked you out with barely any notice, I wouldn't talk to any of them either."

She laughed and scooted closer to the edge of the couch, leaning toward him.

"Is that why you move so much?" His eyes were on the movie in his hands, but the muscles in his neck were tight.

The air whooshed out of her lungs, and she retreated back into the soft cushions of the couch. The instinct to deflect, to lie, to turn the conversation back on him was a battering ram in her brain, pushing out any other thought.

It only took a few breathless moments of watching the way his hands flexed on the DVD box before the urge to lie disappeared. In its place, a warmth filled her chest, loosening the tightness there. All her usual rules didn't seem to apply to Bastien. Keeping her things in her room, making sure everything stayed separate, not letting her sight off her goals was how she'd managed to survive. It was selfish, but necessary.

With Bastien, she didn't want to be selfish anymore. She wanted to give him whatever he asked for.

There's no guarantee he'll give the same back. Or that he even wants me to give that much.

With a twist in her stomach, she gave him the same as she had Austin: the bare minimum. Except the hot rush of blood in her veins was nothing like what she felt around her coworker. "I'm trying to save money to buy a house. That doesn't always align with having the nicest roommates."

"I take it I'm the exception?" Bastien flashed a grin that had her laughing and her stomach twisting again—this time in a good way. When he leaned in closer, his eyes sparkled with the same soft glow she was feeling all over her body.

"Naturally." She tucked her feet underneath her, blood humming in her veins. "We can watch whatever you want to watch. I'm flexible."

Bastien snorted.

"What? You don't think I'm flexible?" Her tone was light, but embarrassment lodged itself in her chest.

"Gabby, this is the first time since you moved in a week ago that you've put any of your stuff in the living room."

Indignant, she pointed to the line of hooks on the wall. "My key is hanging by the door."

He gave her a look that he must use constantly with his four siblings. One that said, "*Are you kidding me right now?*"

She sank back into the couch, not wanting to tell him much, but also not wanting to seem rude. "I just don't want to impose."

It wasn't imposing she was worried about though, not really. It was getting attached. Getting comfortable somewhere, starting to think of it like home.

"Please impose." Bastien held up the stack of movies. "You can start by picking your favorite. Not something you think I'll like. What were you planning on watching today if I hadn't shown up?"

It took a few deep breaths before Gabby could manage to point to *Serenity*.

"This is a great movie. Why are you embarrassed about it?"

She shrugged, done with sharing for the day.

"You know, Anais has this whole system around ice cream and movies." He opened the DVD box. "Sci-fi goes with peanut butter fudge. I should have some in the freezer."

"I'm fine, thanks."

Watching a movie was one thing. Sharing food was a slippery slope toward this feeling like a home and not just a place to stay for a while.

Every home she'd ever had got taken away. Nothing about where she lived ever felt stable. Nothing ever would until she had a house of her own, paid in cash, with her name on it, and an emergency fund in the bank big enough to cover it for a year in case things got bad. But maybe not even then.

"You sure?"

Gabby wrapped the blanket around herself even tighter and

nodded. As he stood up to get it playing on the TV, the familiar fear she'd first felt when he'd helped her move in rushed into her chest, nearly choking her. It wasn't his pity she was afraid of this time, however.

Bastien settled down on the couch a respectful two cushions away, and the air prickled around them. He was close enough to talk about the movie without shouting across the room, but far enough away to make it clear he wasn't trying to make a move or take advantage of the situation.

Except Gabby wanted him to, which terrified her more than anything.

TEN

BASTIEN

Bastien was slicing onions and trying not to cry. It had been a long day at the cabin, and he'd left before Gabby had woken up, just like he had all week. And just like all week, she wasn't home when he got back, so now he was making dinner, planning to eat by himself like he always did. It was like Saturday had been some fever dream, full of laughter and endless movies and debates on the fine line between fantasy and science fiction.

The steady, familiar rhythm of chopping was soothing. He missed cooking for others. He wasn't an amazing cook by any means, but he was decent and liked having people eat his food. When Eli was still in high school, he'd usually come to Bastien's house first before heading home, and Bastien would make him a snack. Or when Dani didn't want to sneak back into their parents' house after a night out, she knew she could crash in Bastien's guest room, and he'd make her pancakes the next day.

This year had been lonely, and Gabby had made him feel less lonely yesterday. Until, halfway through the second movie, he suggested ordering a pizza and she disappeared into her room, mumbling about having articles to read. She was still in there when Jackson came to pick him up to go to the Floodline, and though he'd wanted to knock on her door to invite her, he didn't want to hear the rejection he knew he'd get.

Tonight would probably be the same, but some hopeless, helpless part of him didn't want to give up just yet.

Which explained why, when Gabby walked into the kitchen, Bastien's heart jumped into his throat.

"Hey, right on time." His jaw tightened. What on earth did that mean? "I'm making a big pot of stew. You're welcome to join me."

"Thank you, but I'm not hungry. I just ate with Austin."

The knife in his hand slipped, and he let out a curse as it slit open his thumb.

"Are you okay?" In an instant, Gabby's body was pressed against him, her hand on his. He sucked in a breath, inhaling her shampoo, fruity and warm. There was also the lingering smell of the clinic, of antiseptic and rubber gloves and paper. Even though she was in regular clothes, it clung to her the way it always clung to Anais. It was a comforting smell, one he associated with his family and being safe.

"It's just a surface cut. I've done worse with less." With a regretful tug in his chest, he eased his hand out of her grasp and stuck his thumb in his mouth.

"Bastien!" Her eyes went wide. "That's not sanitary."

She pulled on his arm, and the contact flooded him with almost too much warmth to stay upright. He let it go without any struggle at all.

"You were with Austin?"

She looked up, brow furrowed. "I ran into him when I was out today."

"Oh." The deep inhale he made himself take did nothing to loosen the tightness in his shoulders or soothe the burning in his chest.

Gabby didn't seem to notice his inner turmoil—her only concern was the blood on his thumb. "We'll have to get this cleaned up right away. Have you washed your hands since you got home from working on the cabin?"

"Yes, of course. I was cooking."

"That doesn't mean anything." She clicked her tongue and led him by the arm to the sink and turned on the water. "If you'd seen some of the people I've lived with, you'd understand why I didn't share dishes or cooking with them."

"Is that why?"

"Why what?"

It should have been relaxing to have her wash his hand, but the gentle sudsy strokes of her fingers against his skin were making it hard to remember how to talk.

He swallowed hard. "Is that why you don't want to eat with me or share dishes? Is it just a healthcare worker's concern for cleanliness?"

She frowned and kept her eyes on what she was doing, taking way too much time to dry his hand, but Bastien wasn't about to complain.

"I don't mean it as an insult. I just prefer keeping to myself."

"You didn't yesterday. I had fun." It was the first day off he'd had in... well, he couldn't remember when, but it had been a long time since he'd laid on the couch on a Saturday, watching movies instead of coaching or doing something for the town or working on whatever side project he'd taken on at the last minute.

There was a tremble in Gabby's lips, the barest whisper of a smile there. "I had fun too. It's just not what I'm used to."

"You're used to smelly, disgusting roommates who steal your food and don't wash their hands."

She laughed, and her gaze flitted around the room. He realized what she was looking for. The first aid kit was in the cabinet next to the sink, and he reached with his good hand to pull it out, bringing their bodies closer together, their chests almost touching. She met his eyes as he handed it to her, and she licked her lips slowly.

Their mouths were inches apart, and he tilted his head just

slightly to bring them even closer. He could hear the catch of her breath like a hook behind his ribs, drawing him toward her. His heart pounded in his ears, urging him to ask the question he'd thought about at least a hundred times yesterday, between discussions of favorite Nathan Fillion movies and bad TV show remakes.

Can I kiss you?

Then she stepped back, first aid kit in hand, and the tension broke in a cresting wave. Deflated, he leaned back against the counter, chest aching like the knife had struck him there instead of his thumb.

"Well, I promise I washed my hands." With his other hand, Bastien gestured at the mess on the counter. "I was making dinner for us."

"I can cook for my—"

"I know you can, but why should you if I'm not as terrible as other roommates you have?"

"I don't remember saying you weren't as terrible." Her lip curled, and he felt the spark of the teasing like a shot in the arm, invigorating him.

In so many ways, Gabby was a closed book. One with an intriguing title and enthralling description that had him aching to lose himself in. So far, he'd only read a few pages out of order, and it just sparked his interest even higher.

He chuckled, their faces so close he could smell the summer sunlight sticking to her skin as she carefully applied antiseptic and a Band-Aid to his wound. "So why no dinner?"

"I told you, I already ate."

"How about tomorrow?"

She shook her head again, and his heart dropped somewhere below his knees.

"Am I really that unappealing?"

She started, and with a jolt of guilt, he realized just how angry he'd sounded.

"It's not that."

Hope swirled in his chest.

"I have this stomach issue..." She took a step back, shaking her head. "I have to be careful what I eat. It's a pain, so it's easier to just make my own food. I had some with me earlier, and I ate it in the park while talking to Austin. I always have food with me, just in case."

"What kind of stomach issue?" He licked his suddenly bone-dry lips.

She looked away and started organizing the first aid kit, stacking the Band-Aids into neat little piles and placing the anti-septic in its designated spot. "It's just some weird GI stuff. It's not a big deal."

He raised his eyebrows. If she had to take food with her everywhere, it was a really big deal.

"So tell me what you can eat, and I'll make it."

"It's fine, really. You don't have to do anything special."

"I don't mind. I could probably stand to eat less dairy or whatever."

"If only it were that simple." She rubbed her forehead, each worry line cutting into him like a blade. "It's not like I haven't talked to doctors about it, but it's been hard to figure out triggers. Stress, for sure, but I'm an NP, my job is stressful. Sometimes dairy is fine, other times not. I can eat the same thing two days in a row and one day be fine but the next not."

While his heart squeezed tight, all the other muscles in his body relaxed. This was something he couldn't fix. And not because he wasn't a doctor. The ones she'd seen hadn't even been able to help her, after all. For once, he wasn't deficient in the way he was ninety-nine percent of the time.

All he could do—and he knew he did it well—was listen. "That sounds really hard."

A hesitant smile flitted across her face. "It is."

They stood in silence for a moment, every part of him aching to hold her, to comfort her in some physical way. But she'd wrapped her arms around herself and was leaning into the wall like all she wanted to do was disappear into it.

"Once, when I was watching my little brother and sisters, Clementine dared Eli and Dani to eat fried peanut butter and sardine sandwiches. They both got really sick, and my parents thought they had the flu."

Gabby bit her lip like she was trying not to laugh. "How old were they?"

"I think Eli was in middle school. Dani was maybe a freshman in high school."

"Did you watch them a lot?"

Bastien nodded and leaned back against the counter. "My uncle used to work at the clinic, but he died of an aneurysm when Anais and I were in college. So until she came back after her residency, my dad was running it on his own, just him and a nurse. My mom was in Denver every day, so I'd hang out in the afternoons with the younger ones. They probably could have been on their own at that point, but I didn't mind helping. I started teaching at the high school when Dani and Eli were there and saw them every day."

"That's great that you helped out so much."

He rubbed his hand along the back of his neck. "Well, not sure I helped very much that day. I made the sandwiches."

Now she did laugh, low and throaty and wonderful. "It sounds like you couldn't quite control Clementine." Her arms dropped to her sides.

Bastien felt his mouth pull up in a smile. "I know I'm not supposed to have favorites, but she was like a mini me from the time she could walk. The whole family calls her Minnie."

"That's really cute that you two are so close."

Bastien turned to face the counter, washed his hands, then his knife. Careful to avoid his fingers, he finished chopping the onions he'd abandoned. "I don't know if that's true anymore. When she got back from college and started working at the clinic, we had weekly coffee dates, and everything seemed fine. But then she didn't even tell me she wanted to go into physical therapy instead of general medicine like everyone expected. I mean, who else would understand better than me?"

He turned, waving the knife in his hand, and Gabby let out a little shriek and held up her arm to cover her face.

"Bastien, I'm no longer wondering how it's possible you hurt yourself so much."

"Oh, sorry." He gave her a sheepish grin and turned back to the cutting board. Carrots next, and they required both hands and more concentration. "It's just... It was this major wrench in Anais's plans for the practice, months of tension, of me worrying, and it all gets smoothed away because Anais wants Minnie in her wedding."

Gabby watched him whack at the carrots for a few moments. "I may not have four siblings, but it sounds like you're a little upset that your little sister doesn't need you like she used to."

He stopped cutting and turned to look at her, heart hammering. "That is... a very astute observation."

How had no one in his family noticed this, yet Gabby had seen it in less than a week?

Gabby chuckled. "You sound like such a teacher. Did I get an A?"

"Oh, this was just a pop quiz." He winked. "You're nowhere near ready for the final exam."

"Do I even want to know what that involves?"

"I don't even think my siblings could pass it these days."

He said it like it was a joke, his eyes darting away from her, but Gabby's voice was soft when she replied, "That sounds really hard."

At the echo of his earlier words, he looked up to find her earnest dark eyes staring straight into his. Straight into his soul.

It didn't make sense. He was supposed to be helping her, making her dinner, making life easier however he could. And yet she was standing there, giving him the kind of patient understanding he never expected to get from anyone.

"It is."

While he put the vegetables into the pot, his heart thumping madly, she made her way to the door of the kitchen, hovering just inside.

"Well, I'll let you finish your stew in peace."

"Will you stay and sit with me, even if you can't eat it?" He already knew the answer, but he asked anyway, hope swirling in his chest.

"I can't."

"You can't or you don't want to?"

She bit her lip, the pain and conflict clear in her eyes. "I can't, Bastien, I'm sorry."

Part of his heart left the kitchen with her. Whatever test he'd been taking with Gabby, he'd failed.

ELEVEN
GABBY

Before the salty-sweet smell of hops even hit her nose, Gabby's stomach was in knots.

Two steps inside the Floodline, she turned on her heel. "I'm actually kind of tired. I think I'll—"

"Oh no you don't." Austin put his hands on her shoulder and spun her around. "The office is celebrating Anais, and you are part of the office."

It had been Hunter's idea to go out, when he noticed this was the only Friday evening open for everyone from now until the wedding. By some scheduling miracle, there were no appointments after four, and Dr. Miller was happy to stay at the office on his own, so if they were going to do this, it had to be now.

Normally, this was exactly the kind of thing that Gabby tried to avoid. Not only were drinks expensive, they always led to spilling secrets unintentionally.

Gabby let Austin push her through the crowded bar, wishing she'd at least been able to go home and change. The eyes that landed on her were all familiar, and while most people smiled, some of the women shot her dirty looks at the sight of Austin's hands still on her shoulders.

"Aren't people going to spend all night asking us medical questions?" Gabby maneuvered out from under Austin's touch and slid uneasily onto a stool at the bar next to Jane.

"Probably," said Anais, who had a wide, slightly strained smile on her face.

Gabby felt a tug of warmth for the other woman. Smiling through agony was something Gabby was very familiar with. Somehow, that made it easier to know that someone else felt just as awkward as she did right now.

Austin certainly didn't feel any awkwardness. He was slapping palms with the men behind the counter with one hand while waving to someone on the other side of the room.

"I take it you come here often?" Gabby asked him when he took the stool on her other side.

Austin ran a hand through his dark hair. "Often enough. I like a good pint after work."

"Should I be concerned?"

"Only if you're against ice cream." The bartender put down a container of something chocolatey in front of Austin. "Thanks, Matt."

Matt looked at Gabby expectantly, and she shifted on the stool. "I'm lactose intolerant."

"We have coconut milk ice cream," he said with a wink.

Stomach swirling, she shook her head. "I'll be fine, thanks."

Austin raised a spoon and saluted her with it. "Now was that so hard? Sharing something personal?"

Gabby rolled her eyes. Though she'd kept things professional during their overtime hours together that week, it was hard not to fall under his easy charm and answer some of his questions. There didn't seem to be any harm in talking about what books and movies she liked. Of course, she left out the fact she'd watched one of her favorites with Bastien last weekend, but from the twinkle Austin had in his eyes all week, she bet he somehow knew already.

The knots in her stomach also had her betting he'd guessed

about the almost kiss with Bastien in the kitchen Sunday night. The one she'd been replaying on a loop in her mind all week.

"That's not personal, that's medical." And a lie, one of many she'd probably have to tell tonight. She propped one arm on the bar and leaned her head against her hand. From this position, she could see Austin as well as the crowd behind him. Behind her, she could hear Anais and Hunter and Jane chatting away about table settings and tasting menus. It was noisy but also intimate, and Gabby let herself relax into the moment.

"So I guess it's only fair if you learn something medical about me in return." Austin closed his eyes briefly when the spoon went into his mouth. It was hard not to regret her little lactose lie now. The ice cream did look worth the money, at least.

"I'm perfectly okay remaining ignorant of your medical history."

"Then you get the personal side." He flashed a grin at her, though his eyes were tight. "Exactly two years ago today, my girl-friend told me she was leaving."

"Oh, Austin, I'm so sorry." Gabby reached out a hand to put on his and gave it a squeeze. "I have no idea what to do with that infor-mation, you realize."

He leaned forward on his stool, the noise of the bar a constant buzz around them. Would they be sharing this much if they were back in the break room? Probably not. "You don't have to do anything with it. You just get to know it about me, when almost nobody else does."

"Really?" Her eyebrows shot up. "Not even Anais?"

"She knows something happened. It's why she offered me a job here, back when she was planning on doing a fellowship in Boston and didn't want to leave her dad running things on his own."

"I didn't know that."

Austin shrugged and ate another spoonful. "You never asked."

His words struck her in the chest, not quite a punch but

enough to make her ache. Learning more about her colleagues had never been a priority. A job was for making money, not friends. "If I asked you how many women in this bar you've gone out with, would you answer?"

"Less than half of them." He glanced over his shoulder and squinted. "The other half is afraid to talk to me because of my looks."

"Are you sure it's not because of your humility?" Her lips twitched.

"Considering all my other issues, being aware of the effect I have on people is very healthy."

Gabby laughed, and some of the tension melted away. She was having fun. With coworkers. Outside work. No one had even noticed she wasn't eating or drinking anything. Maybe tonight wouldn't be so bad.

"Bastien, don't you dare!"

At the sound of his name, Gabby's head spun around, heart pounding. Her pulse ticked even higher at the sight of her room-mate-slash-landlord holding his fist above his sister's ice cream. There was a smirk on his face, but then his eyes caught Gabby's and his mouth opened in surprise.

Anais turned to see what her brother was looking at and smiled. "Yes, I know. We finally got her to come out with us. I'm so happy she's here to celebrate with me."

Now it was Gabby whose mouth dropped open in surprise when Anais reached a hand across Jane to squeeze Gabby's. Was it really that important to people to have her around?

Whatever Bastien had been planning on doing to Anais's ice cream, he'd clearly forgotten all about it. He dropped his hand, and his face shifted into one of neutral interest.

"I didn't realize it was the whole office. Hi, Gabby."

"Hi, Bastien."

Gabby could practically feel Austin's knowing smirk behind

her. As casually as she could, she reached her foot over to tap against his, just a little harder than was probably necessary to remind him that not everyone knew about her current living situation.

"Relax." Austin's voice was soft in her ear, his hand firm on her shoulder. From across the bar, Bastien's eyebrows drew together and his lips pulled down. He took a step in their direction but was blocked from getting closer by the haphazard way the stools were arranged next to the bar. Even from this distance, Gabby could see a muscle twitch in his jaw.

"Anyone up for a game of cornhole outside on the deck?" he asked.

Everyone around her groaned. Gabby didn't have time to wonder about this before she heard Austin's voice again, this time louder, for everyone's benefit.

"Gabby, did you know there's a deck? You should check it out. We've all seen it already."

Fire burned in her belly. She didn't know how, but he must know about that almost kiss. It must have been visible on her face as she went about her work.

"You mean we've all gotten tired of Bastien cheating at cornhole," said Hunter with a shake of his head.

Gabby's foot bounced along the bottom rung of her stool. She had to go out there. If she didn't, it would have people asking questions. Damn Austin.

"I mean, if no one else wants to play with him..."

They all groaned again, laughing, and Bastien shook his head with a smile. "I promise I won't cheat."

"He says that every time," Jane said in a not-so-quiet whisper, shaking her gray curls in mock indignation.

"I think I can handle it." With a quick pull to tighten her ponytail, Gabby slid off her stool and raised her chin in a defiant move that gave no hint at just how swirly and squirmy her insides were.

"Ooh," came the chorus of jeers from the group.

Bastien rolled his eyes, but he was smiling. Gabby kept her eyes on him, but he avoided her gaze as he led her through a side door to a small brick-paved deck that overlooked the creek. The night air was chilly for early June, and there was no one sitting at the handful of tables lined up along the edge closest to the creek.

At the sight of the empty deck, Gabby's throat went dry. She hadn't expected to be alone with him. "I'm surprised no one else is out here."

"They will be once the night really gets going. It's still early." He grabbed a bucket with colored beanbags and handed her five blue ones. Their hands brushed, and she shivered.

She looked down at the beanbags, her heart hammering. "I've never played before."

"Don't worry, you'll pick it up fast." He stood behind a line painted on the brick and tossed one of his green bags underhanded toward the board on the other side, where it sailed through a hole. "I noticed you didn't have any ice cream. Is your stomach hurting?"

"What? Oh, yeah." It was easier to let him think it was because of her GI issues and not because of her irrational fear that spending five dollars tonight would ruin her financially.

"I'm sorry. I wish I could help."

A gentle wind tugged at her ponytail, the strands whispering along her neck. "I know."

He held her eyes for a breathless moment, then nodded at the line. "Stand here to throw."

She took a deep breath and stepped up, expecting him to pull away, but he stayed at her side. The sweet smell of sawdust and pine invaded her nose, layered with a cologne that, until a few weeks ago, had been totally unfamiliar.

"Only underhand." He pointed at the board, his arm inches from hers. "Three points if you get it in a hole, one if it lands on the board."

"Right." When he didn't step away, she raised an eyebrow. "Could I maybe get some space to throw?"

In a flash, he was on the other side of the deck, next to the board she was aiming for. She focused her eyes on the holes, which seemed impossibly tiny.

"Is Austin the reason you can't?"

"What?" Her gaze snapped to him right as she tossed, and the beanbag landed a foot to the left of the target.

Bastien rubbed the back of his neck. "The other day, in the kitchen, you said you can't. I thought since you said a few times you had dinner with him, then I saw you with him tonight..."

"Austin's a friend." As her heart squeezed tight, she crushed the remaining beanbags between her palms. "I don't have many."

The muscles in his jaw twitched, and he threw his bag with the ease of someone who did this every day, his eyes fixed on the target instead of her. "Am I your friend?"

She tossed another bag and avoided looking at him. "You're my roommate-slash-landlord."

"Is that why you can't?"

"It's not that I don't want to. It's that I don't even know how." The final bag sailed across the deck, the overfull feeling of having swallowed air stuck in the middle of her chest. "I've spent most of my adult life just trying to get by. I have goals, and I haven't let myself get distracted from them. Any time I have, it ends badly."

There, that was the truth, even if it wasn't very detailed. He didn't need to know about her few failed attempts at dating, her preference for guys without solid jobs or decent backgrounds. If they were a jerk, it made it easier to move on when things inevitably ended.

Bastien was no jerk.

"I can understand that." He tossed his final bag and stood back. "I won."

Well, maybe he was a bit of a jerk. She glanced down at the position of all the bags, then put her hands on her hips. "You cheated."

"Excuse me?" He held a hand to his heart as he strutted in front of his board. "Me? Cheat?"

"You distracted me." Giggling, she kicked one of the bags away. "With your questions and your... eyes."

"My eyes?" He fluttered his lashes at her. "These old things?"

Now she was laughing for real, the sound surprisingly loud in the empty deck. When had she last laughed like this? "Don't pretend you don't know how attractive you are."

"And what about you? The way you keep tugging at that pony-tail is positively Machiavellian."

"You sound like such a history teacher." With a quick yank, she let her hair down. After having it up all day, it felt like she could breathe again now. The laugh had released something inside of her.

"Is that a bad thing?" He took a step toward her.

She shook her head, heart pounding as he took another step. They were nearly chest to chest now. He was broad and strong, as physically impressive as he was intellectually. It didn't always show up, almost like he wanted to hide how smart he was. "Not a bad thing at all."

"Well, good." The words tickled softly on her cheek. "Because that's what I am."

Gabby tilted her head. Something in Bastien's tone was off. "Is there something else you're supposed to be?"

A change swept over his face. From smoldering and intense, it shifted to guarded and forlorn. He took a step back, and she shivered from the absence of him, cool night air racing across her heated skin.

"It's just not what I thought I'd be."

"Do you not like teaching?" The wind blew her hair into her face. By the time she'd brushed it away, he'd retreated all the way to the other cornhole board on the other side of the deck.

"I do." He bent to pick up his bean bags. "It was always my

plan. I was just going to play soccer for a few years before I started."

Her heart squeezed. The ankle injury in college. He'd listed it off like it was just the same as any of his dozens of accidents, but that one mattered more than the others. It had changed his life.

"Do you know why I became a nurse, Bastien?" She bent to pick up her own bags. She looked up to see he'd raised a curious eyebrow.

"You like helping people?"

"To make money." She tossed a bag and released a breath to see it landed on the board, despite how badly her hand was shaking. One point. "Of course I love to help people. Every day, I'm grateful people trust me with their medical issues. But I also have to survive."

She could see the curiosity increase at her choice of words. It felt safer, somehow, to share this bit of her past with him outside, rather than sitting across from the kitchen table at his house. Here they weren't roommates, they were just two people playing cornhole at a bar. They could be just two friends after work. Or two people on a date.

"Would I have made another choice if I'd had it?" This time, the bag she tossed went wide, almost hitting Bastien's legs. He didn't move. "Maybe. But we all make the choices with what life gives us. You can't play soccer, so you teach and coach."

His face was all hard lines and concentration. "And my girlfriend chose to dump me because I teach instead of playing soccer."

So this was his big secret pain. Why he kept the house immaculate and worked all hours for the town and offered a spare room to someone he barely knew. Why he cheated at cornhole.

The bag he tossed landed perfectly in a hole. Three points. Nothing in his expression relaxed. It got even harder, like winning at this game was making up for his imagined inadequacy.

"We can't control what others do, Bastien." The rest of the bags fell from her hands, and she bent to pick them up, tears prickling her eyes. Maybe if she didn't look at him when she said it, it wouldn't hurt as much. "My sister chose to stop talking to me when I became a nurse."

Nope, it still hurt to say out loud. The tears started to fall. In an instant, his warm presence was at her side, helping her pick the beanbags up. He didn't say anything, didn't ask any of the questions she was sure he was dying to. He just grabbed her beanbags, then held out his hand to help her stand.

Wiping her eyes with her sleeve, she took a deep breath and looked down at her hands. If she'd said this much without him reacting badly, maybe he could handle a little more. Not all of it. But more than she'd ever shared with anyone.

"I didn't have the same kind of family as you growing up. We moved around a lot. My mom could never hold down a job for more than a few months because of her issues. Statistically, I shouldn't have even finished high school, but I had a great teacher who encouraged me to try for more. That teacher probably saved my life."

No part of her thought being a teacher was less impressive than being a pro athlete.

"My sister took a different path, followed the example our mother had set. I always hoped that if I had enough money to help her, if she saw what was possible..." She shook her head. "When I told her I wouldn't be using my new degree to get her free drugs, she decided she didn't need me in her life."

He put his hands on her shoulders, rubbing up and down in a very soothing way.

"Please don't tell—"

"I won't. Thank you for trusting me with this." He reached out and tucked a strand of hair behind her ear. The brush of his fingers on her cheek was as intimate as a kiss and just as electrifying to her soul. "It's your life, Gabby. I'm just here to help you live it the way you want to."

This was the third time Bastien Miller had said this to her.

The first time, she'd been sweaty and embarrassed sitting in her car. Her battered and bruised pride hoped she'd never have him see her like that again.

The second time, she'd been anxious at work, her twisted gut worried about the complications of living with her boss's son.

Now when he said it, her broken heart stitched up into something that was almost whole. And all of it was beating for Bastien.

TWELVE

BASTIEN

The morning after the Floodline, Bastien was in bed, staring at the ceiling again, wondering what to do about the woman sleeping in his house.

Just like a few weeks ago, he had no ideas, but the shift in his feelings was like night and day. Brenda was banished from his thoughts, and everything was Gabby.

It had been both a frustration and a relief for Austin and Anais to come out to the deck just moments after Gabby shared that tiny part of her past with him. He'd seen the relief in her eyes when they'd appeared. She'd gone home not long after, and he knew she wouldn't want him to follow, in the same way he knew she'd trusted him not to share what she'd told him. Then Carter Hayes, his friend whose family owned and ran the bar, had insisted on buying Bastien a drink, and he'd gotten home long after Gabby had gone to sleep.

There was a buzz from his phone on the night table. That meant Jackson was leaving his house and would be there in five minutes. Bastien barely had time to get dressed, let alone talk to Gabby—if she was even awake. He was leaving earlier than usual today to get ahead on all the work he couldn't do now that sports camps had started. Working with the kids was always fun, but it made afternoons at the cabin that much more exhausting. They still had to be careful around Bastien's injuries, so work was even slower than expected.

He threw on the same old t-shirt and jeans he'd been wearing all week and made his careful way down the stairs, still skipping the creaky one. When he got to the bottom, his breath caught in his chest.

The light in the kitchen was on.

"Gabby?" He walked in to find her in sweatpants and a long-sleeved t-shirt, sipping her tea and reading a magazine.

She closed it with a quick flip of her wrist, then glanced up at him with a shy smile that broke his heart. "Hi. I couldn't sleep."

"Me neither." His heart pounded in his ears.

"I would have made you coffee, but I don't know how." Her cheeks tinged pink at this. "Always been a tea drinker."

"Oh, don't worry about me." He waved a hand. "Jackson'll be here in a minute. I'll get something on the way to the cabin."

She nodded, her hands tracing the outline of the familiar giant JAMA letters of the *Journal of American Medicine*. He'd watched his parents read it for years, and there was something familiar and homey about seeing it in his own kitchen.

"Will you be at the cabin all day?"

"No, there's a surprise wedding shower for Anais next weekend, so I have to help my sisters with that."

"Oh." She opened the journal again, then her hands stilled on the open pages. "That's nice of them."

"I'm sure you'll be invited. All the staff will."

"How long will you be with them?"

There was something sad in her tone, a trace of regret in the dip of her mouth and the slant of her eyes. The way her finger flicked at a bent corner of a page in her journal was almost sorrowful.

Guilt rippled through him. He couldn't imagine what it would be like if one of his sisters stopped talking to him. The tension over Clementine's career choice had been hard enough, but it wasn't like she'd ever be permanently out of their lives.

"Most of the afternoon, I expect, then there's a planning meeting for the Fourth of July Festival next month."

"So you'll be gone all day?" Her eyes flicked up to his, and with a thunk of his chest, he realized she wasn't thinking about her sister.

She was thinking about him.

There was a honk outside, and he cursed under his breath. "I don't have to do the wedding shower thing. I can tell them I have something..."

Gabby was already pushing back her chair and waving her hand. "You've got a busy day."

"I'll be back in time for dinner, if you want to eat together?" His phone buzzed in his pocket. Jackson was not in a patient mood this morning.

"Yeah, maybe." Gabby was already halfway out of the kitchen. "Have a nice day, Bastien."

Disappointment rippled through him, hot and frustrating. A week ago, he'd felt guilty about spending the whole day lying around watching movies when there were things to get done and people to help. He'd been looking forward to a fully booked weekend.

Now all he wanted was to kick his past self for saying yes to so many things. All he really wanted was to say yes to his roommate, who had walked out of the kitchen without looking back at him.

It was a silent, grumpy kind of morning working on the cabin with Jackson. All they'd managed to do that week was demo the kitchen and the bathroom. The plan for the weekend was to start on the roof. It took a lot of concentration, and there wasn't much room for conversation, which was fine with Bastien. If they worked fast, then maybe there'd be a chance for him to see Gabby before he had to go do wedding stuff.

When they stopped for lunch at Carl's Café, however, his younger sisters showed up moments later, and any hope of seeing Gabby that afternoon disappeared.

"Well, if it isn't my favorite older brother," said Clementine, coming over to the table where he and Jackson had just sat down with their food. Dani was over at the to-go counter, an expectant look on her face. "And my favorite soon-to-be brother."

Bastien sat up straight in his chair, the weariness from that morning gone in an instant. The shower was supposed to be a surprise, so with his sisters here, they'd have to put on a show for Jackson's benefit. "Hey, Minnie. What's up?"

"Just wondering if you're working on the cabin all afternoon?" She had the innocent look that reminded Bastien of the countless pranks she'd play on the youngest two Millers whenever Bastien was left in charge because she knew he wouldn't tell their parents.

Bastien glanced at Jackson, who was digging into a burger like he hadn't eaten in days. "Should we do more today?"

"Hm?" Jackson looked up and smiled at Minnie. "Oh, I just got a text from Anais that there's something wrong with the catering. I should probably go over there with her."

From the counter, Dani put a hand over her mouth to cover her smirk. Bastien bit his lip to stop his own smile. He wondered what Dani had done to mess up the catering, but it was probably better he didn't know.

This kind of mischief was rare these days, and his heart gave a little excited thump to be included in it again. If he wasn't going to be able to spend any time with Gabby today, it would be great to spend it with Dani and Minnie. They were a ton of fun, and it had been ages since they'd been together, just the three of them. Gabby had been right the other day—he was upset his siblings didn't need him like they used to.

"Great." Clementine smiled at the two men. "Sounds like Bastien is free to help Dani and me clear out the attic at Mom and Dad's house."

He raised an eyebrow. Was that the best excuse she could come up with? She was out of practice. "You could at least ask instead of telling me."

Clementine rolled her eyes. "Could you pretty please help us, favorite big brother?"

"I'm your only big brother."

"Until August fifteenth."

Bastien shot a warning glance at her. She was definitely out of practice. Luckily Jackson didn't seem to notice as he concentrated on his food. "I'll be back in time to drive you to the planning meeting tonight."

"Or we can drop him off." Dani came over, jingled her keys, a plastic bag full of takeout around one wrist and a container in another. "I asked Carl for a box for your food."

"Sounds like a plan." There was no point in dragging this out, or they'd ruin the surprise for Jackson. Bastien stood up and grabbed his crutches from where they leaned against the table. With a wave to Jackson, he followed his little sisters out into the parking lot, looking forward to whatever shenanigans they had in mind for the day.

By the time Jackson was driving them back to Bastien's house, it was almost ten. The wedding shower prep with his sisters had been fun, more than fun really, but it had gone on all afternoon. He'd barely been on time for the Fourth of July planning meeting.

It was normally one of his favorite events of the year, but for the third year in a row, all the other faces there were unfamiliar. Since he was the only one who seemed to do anything for Jasper Creek, he'd spent most of the evening bringing a new group of volunteers up to speed. There'd been one perky blond high schooler named Ashleigh who seemed ready to take on the whole project herself. He'd stayed until she'd asked all her questions and he'd heard all her ideas.

As Jackson weaved through the silent streets of Jasper Creek, Bastien finally let thoughts of Gabby consume him. He shouldn't have needed her words to remind him that he could make a huge impact on students as a teacher. It was one of the things he liked best about his job. But to hear what a difference it had made to Gabby, to have her share that part of her past when it was clear she was used to keeping everything to herself... she'd helped him see his life differently.

A streetlamp flashed a quick beam of brightness into the car. It was so late she'd probably be asleep. Another chance missed to spend time with her. The disappointment was thick in his throat.

Every new piece of information he learned about her overturned the preconceived ideas he had about her. And about his own life. Like stumbling across profound quotes without context on social media, he'd gotten a taste and now was starving for more, without knowing how to get it.

He was also just starving, period. As if to agree, his stomach let out a growl just as they pulled into his driveway. The house was dark. He let out a sigh.

Jackson raised an eyebrow. "We should have stopped for food. You want me to turn around?"

"No, I'll be fine. Thanks again for coming tonight."

"Hey, this is what I signed up for when I moved here." He gave his shoulder a shove. "Don't tell me you're getting sick of me."

"Not at all. Now get home before Anais finds something new to yell at me about." Walking up the front path, heart heavy, Bastien was overwhelmed by the jealousy simmering just below the surface. He was happy for Jackson, so happy. He was grateful, so grateful, that he was here to help him.

But he also hated his friend, just a little. Just enough to make Bastien feel like a terrible person. Just enough to remind him why nothing he did—the town festival, the cabin, the wedding shower, giving Gabby a place to live—would ever be enough to balance out his selfishness.

He opened the door as quietly as he could, even though he knew that with Gabby's bedroom on the other side of the house, she wouldn't hear it.

Leaving his crutches by the door, he hobbled to the kitchen, keeping the weight on his right heel to avoid putting his toes on the ground. The injury was healing well, but if he wanted to walk down the aisle at Anais's wedding without crutches, he'd have to be extra careful.

Thinking of the wedding again took away what little appetite he had, but he kept going into the kitchen. Too many years as an athlete wouldn't let him end a day without making sure he had the calories needed. Even if they would be mostly empty calories in the form of the ice cream Gabby hadn't wanted to share the other day. He understood better why she did that, but it didn't make the rejection any easier.

When he flipped on the light in the kitchen, there was a plate on the table, covered with another plate. He inhaled sharply and rubbed his eyes. Now he did put his foot on the floor to get to the table as fast as possible. The ache in his toe and ankle was a sharp reminder that he hadn't fully healed.

He sat down in front of the plate, a lump in his throat the size of a soccer ball. There was a note on top of it, in loopy, unfamiliar handwriting that he soaked in, memorizing every curve and swoop.

I hope you had fun with your sisters. I thought you might be hungry when you got home, so I made extra. —G

The lump in his throat made its way into his chest, where it burned bright and hot, more satisfying than anything he'd ever eaten.

THIRTEEN
GABBY

Gabby stood at the entrance to the Miller family's house and triple-checked that her tights were straight. The invitation to Anais and Jackson's wedding shower came very last minute, just two days earlier. Even with Bastien's heads-up, there'd barely been time to get a gift, let alone a new outfit. She was in the same dress as she'd worn for their Easter party and prayed no one would notice.

Or notice that it fit tighter around her belly than it had back then. Her gut had been behaving itself recently, but that meant eating more. If she bought new clothes every time she went up or down a few sizes, she'd barely have anything in her savings. So a too-snug dress and tights that dug into her waist were what she had on today.

Taking as deep a breath as possible given the less than ideal clothing situation, she stepped onto the porch and knocked on the door. It was opened barely a second later by a young raven-haired woman who could only be Danielle, the youngest Miller sister. Gabby knew she was going to start med school at Centennial U in the fall, but that was about it.

Oh, and that she'd thrown up once after eating a peanut butter and sardine sandwich.

It was probably better not to bring that up today.

"Gabby!" Before she knew what was happening, she was wrapped up in the arms of the mini future doctor. Almost a half-foot shorter than Gabby, it was surprising just how strong the embrace was. Danielle's voice lowered to a whisper. "You have to help me. Austin took over the snack table, and I don't have it in me to scold him."

Stepping out of her arms, Gabby raised an eyebrow. "He's not going to bite."

A red flush crept across Danielle's cheeks, and Gabby bit the inside of her cheek to keep from laughing. This was what Austin had been trying to tell her the other day. His looks certainly hadn't made things harder for him, but at least he was conscious of the effect it could have on others. Apparently not even the Miller women were immune.

"I'll take care of it." Gabby flashed her a reassuring smile. "Lead the way."

The Easter picnic had been outside, so this was the first time Gabby was seeing the interior of the house. She wasn't sure what she'd been expecting, but she wasn't surprised to see the homey, cozy kind of Colorado cabin you could plaster all over social media.

She was surprised, however, when she got to Austin and the snack table that was causing so much stress.

"Doritos, really?" Gabby raised an eyebrow at the five different kinds on display. "Is this what Anais would like?"

"Hey, this wasn't my idea. It was your room—Bastien's idea." Austin flashed her an apologetic look. "I am just setting it up per his instructions."

This was a surprise party, so Anais and Jackson weren't there yet. She didn't know when they were going to arrive or how long she had to fix this. A knot wrapped itself around her stomach, tighter than a shoelace left in the rain, wet and impossible to unravel.

"Where is he?"

Austin waved in the direction of the kitchen.

She sighed. "Where can I put my gift?"

He tilted his head, giving her an inscrutable look. "I told you they didn't need anything."

He had, and she hadn't believed him, naturally. Even if she'd never been to a wedding shower—or a wedding—Gabby knew gifts were an important part of the celebration. Frantic searching online had revealed countless ideas for gifts, and she'd convinced herself that if she didn't spend at least fifty dollars, they'd be upset. She ended up spending one hundred dollars on something called a wine-preserving stopper. She didn't even know if they drank wine. The anxious clench at the unplanned expense hadn't relaxed until she'd seen her paycheck come through the day before. There was still a nervous twist that would stay there until Anais and Jackson opened it and she knew that she'd chosen right.

Or maybe I should have listened to Austin?

Tears were now threatening to well as she swallowed away the tightness in the back of her throat. "Well, I got something. Where can I put it?"

"Put what?"

Gabby turned, and Bastien was standing at the entrance to the living room, looking impossibly handsome in a green shirt that exactly matched his eyes. Eyes that were now darting between her and Austin with a fiery glint. Without knowing why, she took a step back from Austin, even though they weren't standing that close together. From what Bastien had said at the Floodline, some part of him was jealous of her coworker.

And some part of her really liked that.

This, apparently, didn't go unnoticed by Austin, who suddenly had a smug grin on his face. "Gabby brought something for Anais and Jackson. I told her she didn't have to."

She smacked his arm. "And I said I wanted to, then Austin was no help at all. I hope they like it."

"I'm sure they will." Bastien took a step forward and lowered his voice. "You could've asked me for help."

She bit her lip. Was he mad? "You haven't been around."

He'd been gone more than usual this week. Sending a text message seemed like a ridiculous idea since they lived in the same house. She should be able to talk to him. But he'd gotten home after she went to bed every night that week, and was gone in the morning when she woke up.

It must be because of the food she'd made him. Her anxiety crept higher, grabbing hold of her heart and squeezing. She thought making him dinner was a good way to show him she could be open to sharing more if he wanted, but being scarce all week was clearly his way of saying that he wasn't interested. That everything she'd told him made him realize she wasn't someone he wanted to spend time with.

Bastien's eyes flicked to Austin, who stared back, that self-assured smile still on his face. "Don't worry, I won't tell anyone about your living arrangement."

"What living arrangement?"

The color drained from Austin's face as Danielle walked in.

While furious glances passed between the two men, Danielle's question hung in the air. They were saved from answering when Clementine appeared. She gasped at the snack table and turned to face her brother with a glare for the ages. "*Bastien*. You had one job this week. Did you seriously spend it hunting down eight different flavors of Doritos?"

Gabby put a hand to her stomach, breathing through her nose in short, sharp beats. It wasn't the belly breathing she knew she should be doing, but her brain was jumping from thought to thought too fast to settle on anything remotely helpful.

"What living arrangement?" Danielle repeated, hands on her hips, looking from Bastien to Austin to Gabby.

While Austin looked at the ceiling, his lips pursed, Bastien was looking at Gabby. He was giving her the choice to tell them, if she wanted to.

With a deep breath that only released a fraction of the tension in her gut, she lifted a shoulder, faking nonchalance, then let out the air slowly. "I'm renting Bastien's guest room for the summer."

"Oh." Danielle's brow furrowed, and she exchanged a puzzled glance with Clementine, who shrugged. "Why is that a big deal?"

"It's not," said Bastien, picking up a bowl of bright red chips and popping one in his mouth. The explosive crunch echoed in the cozy room. "It's just Gabby shouldn't have to share personal details like where she lives if she doesn't want to."

"Thanks, Captain Obvious." Clementine rolled her eyes, then noticed Austin's bemused smirk and flushed. "They'll be here in fifteen minutes. Can you please fill this snack table with something actually edible for humans?"

Within seconds, the room was empty and Gabby was alone. The anxious knot in her stomach hadn't totally disappeared, but all the other tension in her body lifted away. She looked down at her feet; she could have sworn she was floating on air.

Nobody cared that she was renting from Bastien. It wasn't a big deal. She wasn't in trouble, she wouldn't get fired, she didn't have to move.

She was still standing there, floating, when Bastien came back in and smiled. Only it wasn't just a smile, it was like his entire face lit up from the inside, the joy almost palpable in the way it radiated from his skin.

"That went well," he said.

He was still a few feet away from her, standing by the table with a tray of mini sandwiches balanced on one hand, but she felt the words like he'd brushed them against her cheek. She shivered, shaking out her shoulders and neck as the last of the tension left her. He frowned and put down the tray. In a heartbeat, he was in front of her.

"Are you cold?" He reached up his hands as if to lay them on her shoulders, then paused. His hands dropped to his side, and she felt the lack of them, like they'd been wrapped around her for hours. This whole time, he'd been protecting her in the only way she'd allowed him. "I can turn up the heat."

"I'm fine." A smile tugged at her lips. "I'm just relieved. I was really worried it would be a problem that I'm renting from you."

"I didn't think it would be, not really, but you wanted to keep it to yourself, which is fine." Somewhere in the house a door slammed, and the excited chatter of Danielle and Clementine floated through the air. They were alone, but not for long.

"Thank you. It's hard for me to share personal things."

There was a pause, and he looked away. "You shared it with Austin."

A snort that would have been embarrassing a few weeks ago flew out of her. "He guessed, Bastien. He's very smart."

"And attractive."

"Not as attractive as you." Heat rushed to her face at this, and she looked away. From across the paltry twelve inches that separated them, she could hear him swallow hard.

"So you're saying I don't have to be worried about Austin?" His voice was low, unsteady, more uncertain than she'd ever heard him.

Eyes still on the floor, she shook her head. It should be easier to talk to him now, shouldn't it?

The closeness of him made it even harder to focus, to form words. Her tongue was heavy in her mouth. When she parted her lips to take a deep breath, he brought his hand up to brush her hair back from her face. At the first gentle graze of his fingers, she dragged her eyes up to meet his. They were inches from hers, intensely green like the trees lining the street outside, more brilliant than the sun shining through the windows.

"Can I kiss you, Gabby?"

Heart in her throat, she shook her head again. "Not here."

Nobody might have cared if she was renting his room, but

they'd certainly have thoughts if they saw them kissing in the middle of a party for Anais and Jackson.

"Soon." His voice was a rumble in her ear that touched every nerve in her spine. She nodded, and the slow smile that spread across his face sent lightning streaking across her skin. It was a single word that held more promise than the ocean had water.

She took a step back, barely daring to breathe.

Soon.

FOURTEEN
BASTIEN

The party dragged on for hours, Bastien's mood passing from euphoric bliss to a surly misery that, if Clementine's pointed looks were any indication, he was doing a terrible job at hiding.

If there were anything in his power to speed things up, to make time go faster, to get everyone to just stop talking so he could leave and do the one thing he'd been thinking about for weeks, then he would have done it fifteen times already.

Instead, he smiled and laughed and talked with the same people he saw every day of his entire life, while casting secret glances at the one person he wanted to be alone with.

It was Austin, of all people, who finally gave him the out he desperately needed.

"Why don't we let the Millers have their house back and take this party to the Floodline?" the handsome doctor bellowed around six in the evening, long past the scheduled end time of the party.

His suggestion was met by cheers from the assembled crowd, including Isabelle and Carter Hayes and their cousin Matt. They'd normally be working at the bar but had taken the afternoon off to come to the party. Isabelle was Anais's oldest friend, and in a perfect world, Bastien would have fallen for her in high school and made things simpler for himself.

Looking around, he wondered if this would have been a party for him and Isabelle if he hadn't met Brenda. Then his eye caught Gabby's, and his chest filled with something golden and wonderful and he didn't care about the party anymore. He just wanted to be anywhere else with the first person in years who reminded him just how important he was to people, while also making him feel like there was more to life than serving the needs of others. Like maybe there was more to him.

Everyone tossed their cups and plates in the trash cans Bastien had been emptying every so often all afternoon, then made their way to the door. His parents were there to thank everyone, with wide smiles but a clear weariness in their eyes.

"I can stay to help clean up," he said as guilt threatened to crush the simmering excitement at the sight of Gabby lingering just outside the door, waiting for him.

"Go have fun, Bastien." His mom reached up to plant a kiss on his cheek. It was a rare thing, both the kiss and command to enjoy himself. Light swelled in his chest. "And make sure your sisters don't have too much fun."

Like a popped soccer ball, he deflated in an instant. "Of course."

Because it was never just about him, was it? He was the one who had to think of others, never of himself.

With a heavy heart, he joined Gabby in the front yard, observing the mass exodus of people and cars on the narrow street. In the middle of it all, Anais beamed up at Jackson, laughing and talking with everyone as they sorted out the logistics of who would ride with who.

"She looks really happy," Gabby said quietly. "But I thought she was going to run away when she came in and saw everyone standing there."

Bastien shook his head. "Oh, she loved it. She was probably just worried about not being dressed right."

Gabby chuckled. "That's what I was worried about actually."

"You look great." All afternoon his eyes had been drawn by the swish of her hem against her legs, the way the dress hugged every curve. "Were you able to eat anything?"

The corners of her lips tugged up. "Yes. It's been a good day."

As if he could sense that Bastien and Gabby were finally having a private moment, Austin appeared at the door. "Can I give the two of you a ride?"

"I drove here, so I'm all set." Gabby gave him a smile.

"I came with Minnie and she..." Bastien looked around at the now empty street in front of the house and let out a hum of annoyance. "She left."

A featherlight touch of Gabby's hand on his arm evaporated whatever grumpiness he had toward his younger sister. "I'll get us there. You go ahead, Austin."

"Take your time." With an arrogant smile, he walked off, leaving the two of them alone on the porch.

They waited until he drove off before making their way to her car, the only one left on the street. It looked just as old and broken down as it had a few months ago. A tremble of hopeful anxiety threaded through him. Maybe it wouldn't start. Then they wouldn't have to meet everyone else at the bar.

Gabby seemed to pick up on his unspoken thoughts. "It got me here okay, so we should be fine."

The thrill of delight when it didn't start, however, was quickly stamped out by the tears pooling in the corner of Gabby's eyes.

Maybe she didn't want to be alone with him. Maybe she wanted to keep partying with Austin and the others.

"Hey, it's okay." His hand was already on the door. "I'll go ask my parents if we can use their—"

"No, don't!" She grabbed his arm, and he stilled. "I'm so embarrassed right now."

"Why?" He gestured at the street, though it was empty of cars right now. "Nobody cares what kind of car you have. Not in Jasper Creek."

"It's not that." She took a few inhales, her hand still on his arm. The heat of it was not quite enough to distract him from how upset she was, and he put his own hand on top. This seemed to slow her breathing a bit, and a rush of relief flooded into him. He was helping, somehow, even if he didn't understand how it could be enough to just be there with her. Like he was enough, without doing anything special.

"I just don't like asking for help," she said.

"I get that."

Her eyes were still watery, but there was the flicker of a smile. "I know you do. That's why I can tell you about it."

"Do you want to walk?"

"Not all the way to the Floodline. Not in these shoes."

"So what do you want to do?"

"Let's go home."

Warmth filled him at the words.

Home. With Gabby.

Had anything ever felt so right?

It was almost as far to his house as it was to the Floodline, but Bastien wasn't going to be the one to mention that. They left her car and started walking, the whispering silence of the leafy trees above their heads stretching between them.

"That was fun." Gabby's voice held a smile that touched him in the middle of his chest. "Not like the Easter picnic."

"That was my parents' thing. This was all Minnie and Dani."

"And you."

He shrugged that away. "I was just in charge of snacks."

"And cleaning, and keeping the ice stocked, and probably a hundred other things I didn't even notice."

He looked up at the trees lining the street and rubbed the back of his neck. "You notice a lot more than most people."

"I think because they've always had it, they don't realize how lucky they are."

"And you feel lucky?"

She reached over and squeezed his hand. She might as well have reached into his chest and wrapped her fingers around his heart. "Every day."

Words did not want to come in answer to that, so they walked in silence, hand in hand, for a few minutes. The early-evening sun was hitting the trees in just the right way to make them all sparkle and glow.

"You don't have to be jealous of Austin, you know."

He turned, chest tight. "I know, but I think part of me always will be." Deep breath. Might as well share it all with her. "Not because of you. Because of me. He's the brother doctor Anais didn't get with me."

"I think she's pretty happy with the brother she has." There was that squeeze of his hand again, a direct link to the organ behind his ribs pumping blood twice as fast as it normally did.

"He's more important than I am."

Now she stopped and turned to face him, the hand not holding his on her hip. "What on earth does that mean? Bastien, you are incredibly important to your family. Do you really not see that?"

He shrugged, not wanting to let her see how much it meant to actually hear the words, to feel them in his core the way he never had before. Actions spoke louder than words, though, and everyone from his mom to Brenda had shown him over and over how unimportant he was.

He felt important to Gabby.

"Bastien." She tugged his hand and he looked at her. They were underneath the long line of oak trees on a quiet side street, still two blocks from their house. His house, he corrected himself. Despite himself, he'd begun thinking of it like theirs. Now that his family knew she was living there, that last barrier to hoping for something more had been broken.

He wanted more. He wanted her so much it hurt. He wanted her to feel safe and loved and to never have to worry about anything. This was more than the general helpfulness he felt for everyone else. This was intense, right in the middle of his chest, like he was being crushed and the only way to get rid of that pressure was to see her shoulders relax, to see the lines around her mouth smooth out and turn into smile creases instead.

"You don't have to be jealous of Austin."

She'd said the same thing only moments before, but this time, he was looking into her eyes when the words passed over her smooth, pink lips. Her tongue darted out to lick the bottom one, and the pressure in his chest increased tenfold, making it hard to breathe.

He wanted her so much.

Time for more honesty. She hadn't run yet, and maybe she was the one person who never would. "I'm jealous of anyone who gets to spend all day with you."

The pink tinge to her cheeks was barely visible in the shade of the trees, but he soaked it up. It was selfish, wanting to be the only one to make her react this way. Selfish to be thinking of what he wanted on the same day he'd celebrated his sister and best friend.

"You get to spend all night with me." The pink turned scarlet. "I mean, shoot, that's not what I meant—"

He laughed and brought up a hand to tuck her hair behind her ear, the golden strands dappled with sunlight filtering between the leaves of the trees above them. The street was surprisingly quiet for a Saturday evening. No cars passing, no families out walking in the warm summer sunshine. It was just him and Gabby, alone in the shade of the oaks he'd walked past his entire life.

Maybe just this once, he could be selfish.

"I know what you meant. I like coming home, knowing you're there. Even if you're asleep. It's nice to not have an empty house."

Her lips twisted down a little at this. "So you could just have one of your sisters come be your roommate."

"They have their own lives to live." The words only stuck a little in his throat. It felt selfish to want something for himself when his whole life he'd been thinking about what they needed. "I think I'll have to get used to them not needing me anymore if I want to start living my own life."

With Gabby, if she wanted that.

"That sounds like a good idea."

"You know what else sounds like a good idea?" He was inches away now, could see each eyelash and freckle, feel the gentle whisper of her breath across his skin. "If we kissed right now."

"Oh yeah?" Her tone was daring, but her eyes were eager. "I think I'd like that."

When he brought his lips to hers, he could feel her smile. He could feel himself smile, and every tiny intake of breath that they shared as their kiss deepened and they wrapped themselves up even tighter.

Nothing had ever felt this perfect. No one had ever felt this right. The heat of her mouth and the dance of his tongue on hers was beyond anything he'd ever felt with... His brain couldn't even think of the name of anyone else he'd ever been with. It was just Gabby. Only Gabby.

He could have stayed like that forever, but she pulled back with a slight inhale, her arms still wrapped around him.

"We should probably not be doing this here."

It took his fuzzy brain almost a full minute to process the unspoken request in her words. All he wanted to do was to keep kissing her, and was having a hard time understanding why they'd stopped.

"Outside?"

Her teeth slid over her bottom lip and part of his chest caved in. "In the middle of the street."

"Then let's go home."

"Home."

Had a single word ever sounded so wonderful?

FIFTEEN
GABBY

"Did you have a good weekend?" The smile that accompanied Austin's question could only be described as devious.

Gabby bent to put her Tupperware full of lunch in the fridge. The chilly air helped cool her cheeks.

"Yes. And you?" She peeked over the edge of the fridge door, fussing with the half-empty bottles of salad dressing that were in there. "This expired last year. We should throw it away."

"Don't be difficult." Austin crossed over to her and grabbed the offending bottle. Without even looking, he tossed it behind him and it landed in the trash can by the door.

Gabby's eyebrows shot up. "That was impressive. Did you play basketball in school?"

"Don't change the subject." His hand hovered over her shoulder in an unspoken question. When she nodded her permission, he moved her gently away from the fridge and into a seat. He sat across from her, arms folded across his chest. "You never showed up at the Floodline. Neither did Bastien."

Her stomach twisted. "Did anyone notice? Were they all talking about it?"

"No." Austin flashed her a smile, this one gentler, though it still held the twinkle of mischief around the edges. "They were busy with Danielle's karaoke version of the entire *Mamma Mia* movie."

"The Floodline has karaoke?"

"They do if you're Danielle and you tell Matt Hayes you want to sing."

A chuckle slipped out, and the tightness in her belly unclenched. "I'm sorry I missed it. Did Anais and Jackson have a good time?"

"Good enough. If Anais had her way, she'd drive to Vegas and get married tonight and not tell anyone."

This surprised Gabby a little. Bastien's view of his sister seemed at odds with how Anais's friends saw her. It made sense, though, that he would see his sister as competition, as getting everything he wanted. Like the attention he so desperately craved, did so much to get, and yet they all took him for granted. Warmth bloomed in her chest. She could give that to him. It wasn't much, but maybe it could be enough.

"Doesn't she want to celebrate with her family?"

"Yeah, but this is turning into something way bigger than she planned. This wedding shower was not something she wanted. It's why I said you didn't have to worry about a gift."

"Well, that's nice to know you weren't trying to embarrass me." Gabby shifted in her chair.

"Did you really think I would do that?"

She bit her lip and looked away. "I don't know. Maybe?"

When she looked back, Austin had a pained look on his face. "I know I joke around a lot, but I do that because you're my friend. You know that, right?"

"You're my friend." She tried out the words, still a little awkward in her mouth. "I don't really have many."

"I'd guessed as much, yes." His smile was gentle now, no hint of his usual all-knowing smirk, the brilliance in his eyes was warm and comforting. "I don't know why you don't have many though."

Gabby stood up. "I need to get some tea."

Austin waved her back down. "Fine, fine, that was too far. You don't have to tell me anything you don't want to. I'm just interested in people."

"So am I, but I don't notice every little detail the way you do."

It would make her life easier if she could read people the way he did. Then she'd know that they were safe, that she could trust them. Things would go faster if she could take down all her walls with any level of confidence.

"It's only because I'm so desperate to escape into someone else's life." Austin sank back in his chair, his eyes focused on something far away in the distance.

A tendril of warm familiarity wrapped itself around Gabby's heart. There was so much more to Austin, and it seemed like the genius doctor didn't even realize it. "Wow, that's dark for someone so pretty."

He laughed at this. "I think dark recognizes dark. But the Millers are all light. It's been good for me to work here. I think it'll be good for you."

"It already has been." She put a cautious hand over his and squeezed. "I have a friend now."

One eyebrow shot up at a teasing angle. "And a very handsome roommate."

Pursing her lips, Gabby pulled her hand away and stood up again, then fetched a mug from a cabinet. With her back turned, she was able to give him a little more of what he so clearly wanted. "Well, maybe he's more."

"Really? I hadn't guessed."

When Gabby turned back to glare at him, the smirk was firmly in place, and she couldn't help but laugh.

She put her mug of water in the microwave. "Alright, smarty-pants. You caught me."

"So I guess that takes care of your living situation."

A shot of panic sliced into her chest. "What?" The microwave beeped, but she ignored it.

He leaned back in his chair and frowned. "Well, you're already living with him. That's a milestone few couples even get to. It should be smooth sailing from here on out."

The beeping was insistent now. "But I only have a lease until the end of the summer."

Austin raised an eyebrow. "And leases can't be extended? Or transformed into a cohabitation between two people in a relationship?"

In a relationship. Her stomach fluttered.

"The whole point of living somewhere cheap is to save for a house on my own." She turned and finally opened the microwave. The mug was hot in her hand, but she held on to it tightly. "Of my own."

Nope, the words still sounded off.

"Have you talked with Bastien about this?"

"It's been, like, two days since this even became anything. Why would we even talk about stuff like that?" The usual box of tea she liked was almost empty. She'd have to ask Hunter to order more. "But yes, he knows I'm saving for a house. Why would that change just because we went from roommates who barely see each other to roommates who make out?"

That last part slipped out, and she could feel a flush heat her face.

"Gabby and Bastien sitting in a tree..." Austin whispered with a wicked grin.

Heart racing, she threw away the empty box of tea at him and he caught it with one hand. "What about you?"

"What about me?"

"Visit anyone on my street lately?"

He leaned back, and the corner of his mouth twisted. "Do you really care?"

"Well, yeah." She smoothed her hand over her sleek ponytail. "Dark recognizes dark. I can tell you're lonely. If you need to seek comfort, as long as you're being safe about it—"

He held up a hand. "Are you seriously about to have 'the talk' with a former emergency room doctor?"

She rolled her eyes. "You know doctors are the worst patients. You could be ignoring some very basic rules."

"Don't worry. I'm following all the rules, and then some extra ones I put in place myself."

Curiosity bloomed, but she bit back the endless questions that she knew he probably wouldn't answer. No sense giving him more opportunities to turn things back on her.

"Alright, keep your secrets for now." She lifted her mug to him in salute. "We have extended hours tonight. I'll get my answers one way or another."

She left the room with his laugh booming in her ears and her body feeling lighter than it had in ages.

A few hours later, however, the familiar anxiety was back. Knowing Austin would be as ruthless looking for answers as she would be, Gabby ducked into the bathroom and sent a quick text to ask Bastien if he wanted to meet her for dinner at the café. Having a reason to escape the second the last patient was out the door would keep Austin from prying too deeply into this glittery new thing between her and Bastien.

Unfortunately, the same generous, sweet man that sent jittery electricity through her veins was also generous with the town.

He answered with a string of sad faces.

I HAVE A MEETING FOR THE FOURTH OF JULY TONIGHT. I CAN DUCK OUT EARLY THOUGH.

NO. She shook her head as she tapped out her reply. I'LL SEE YOU AT HOME.

Disappointment filled her chest, followed swiftly by dread. One way or another, Austin was getting his questions answered tonight.

As the summer sun dipped behind the mountains surrounding Jasper Creek, Gabby found herself sitting across from Austin at Carl's Café.

"I still say I can eat by myself at home." Gabby folded her arms across her chest.

"Nonsense. It's my treat."

"I can also pay for myself."

"Then how would I guilt you into answering my questions?"

She rolled her eyes, the tickle of a laugh touching the edges of her lips. Sometimes he was too charming for his own good.

There was a beep in her bag, and she took the opportunity to duck under the table to retrieve it. The smile that spread across her face was hard to hide as she straightened up.

Austin waggled his eyebrows. "Is it your roommate?"

"No, my real estate agent."

"Oh?"

With only the smallest of hesitations, Gabby flipped around the phone to show him. "I only just reached out yesterday. She already found something in my price range."

If Austin had any thoughts on that very low range, or on the giant crack still in her phone screen from weeks ago, he kept them to himself. Just like Gabby knew he would. The relief and comfort of having a friend was like a balm to aching muscles. Of course, she could keep going without it, but life was so much more enjoyable with it.

"It looks cute." Austin bit into his burger. "Will you go see it with Bastien?"

It was like he knew the one question she wouldn't want to answer.

She shoved her phone back into her bag. "Why would he need to see it? He's not the one buying it."

He got a look on his face, but before he could say anything, someone called out to them.

"Hi, Gabby. Hi, Austin." Clementine waved, handed some cash to Carl for her order, and walked over.

"Hi. I thought you were at school during the week?" Gabby asked.

With an eye roll that made her look just like Bastien, Clementine sighed. "Anais and Mom asked me to drive up to help with something for the wedding they swore couldn't wait until this weekend, and Bastien wasn't around."

Something sharp prickled along Gabby's spine, but she just nodded.

"How are the extended hours going?"

"Really well." Austin smiled, and Gabby noticed the quick jump of Clementine's chest as she inhaled sharply at the sight of his dazzling grin.

While it was still understandable why women reacted this way around him, Gabby only saw her charismatic friend with some loneliness lingering just below the surface. She wanted all the good things in the world for him and hoped it could happen with someone sweet. Someone like Clementine, but who didn't visibly tremble when he flashed his smile.

"We might keep them through the fall." Gabby saved the younger woman from more of his effusive attractiveness. "They've been really popular."

"That's great. You must be looking forward to a break next week."

Breaks always meant less money, but for once she was actually looking forward to it. The Fourth of July was the following Wednesday and Bastien had been talking about it nonstop. "Oh yeah. It'll be nice to see how Jasper Creek celebrates."

"Bastien does a great job with the festival." Austin put just the slightest weight on the name, his lips turned up a fraction of an inch.

Of course Austin would bring him up. Gabby pursed her lips and held back the impulse to kick him under the table. There wasn't a tablecloth, so it would be too obvious.

"Oh, totally. This town is the most important thing to him." Clementine shook her head. "I don't know how he does it all."

Gabby found herself biting back a sharp reply. He did it by ignoring his own needs. By putting the town and its residents ahead of his own health. Surely, his own family would be the first to notice that? His toe and ankle had just barely healed, but he still was running the camps and working on the cabin. If Clementine was complaining she'd been called in tonight instead of her brother, then it seems like everyone just expected him to do it all, no matter what.

"Will you be there?" Clementine asked Gabby, then her eyes flicked to Austin.

"Yes, we both will," replied Austin, his voice at a lower pitch than usual. Gabby was tempted again to kick him. If he didn't turn down the charm a notch on Clementine, the girl would melt. "Looking forward to it."

"Great. I'll see you there." Carl called her name from the counter. Her food was ready. She looked back briefly, then gave them both a smile. "Enjoy your dinner."

She waved and headed out. Austin's eyes followed her for a moment, then fixed on Gabby, laser focused.

"I guess no one in his family knows about you two." He sipped his drink. "The festival could be a good place to make things public."

"It's nobody's business." Just like her living situation was private, she wanted to keep this private. It was too stressful to think about Anais or Dr. Miller treating her differently. It was one thing for Austin to have figured things out, quite another to have the entire Miller clan involved.

"It will be when he's glued to your side all day."

"I'm sure he'll be busy with the festival." Gabby moved some leaves of her salad around her plate. Austin had said it was his treat, but she hadn't wanted to get something too expensive. "You'll have to show me around."

"I'm happy to do that, if needed." His eyes traced the pattern she was making with her lettuce. "But I don't think it will be."

"You heard his sister. Nothing's more important than this town to him."

Austin didn't say anything, but he had that smug smile on his face again. "We'll see."

SIXTEEN

BASTIEN

For the first time in almost ten years, Bastien didn't rush out the door on the morning of the Fourth of July. There was still a to-do list a mile long and a dozen unanswered messages on his phone, but he ignored all of them to sit just a few minutes longer with Gabby on the couch, drinking coffee and watching the sun rise through his back windows.

"I can go with you to help." From her position snuggled against his chest, she yawned, and he laughed.

"You need to sleep. Those longer hours at the clinic are taking a toll."

"And what about you? You've been going nonstop all summer."

His chest squeezed at her concern. It was no different from any previous summer, except now he had someone at home who noticed everything he did. "I didn't work on the cabin at all this week."

"Only because Jackson had to do wedding stuff."

It was true. It hadn't been intentional, but Jackson had the wedding in addition to the festival, so they both agreed a week off wouldn't be a bad idea. The nagging sense of failure Bastien had expected from a decision like that was nowhere to be seen. Probably because he'd spent that extra time with Gabby. They had breakfast together in the mornings, he took her lunch at noon, and walked home with her after work.

So far, no one in his family had noticed, which was a miracle in and of itself. Today would probably be too hard to hide his need to spend every minute with her, so he wanted extra time this morning, just the two of them.

"Are you complaining about seeing your roommate-slash-landlord too much?" He reached down to tickle between her ribs. This set her off giggling, but also thrashing and shrieking so much that the blanket wrapped around her fell away. The flash of the rose tattoo on her shoulder drew his eye, just like it had weeks ago that first Saturday he'd watched movies with her.

There was a heavy silence as his eyes traced the edges of her tattoo. His arms were framing her body with his hands still on her sides, their faces inches apart. He could hear her staggered breathing, feel the pitter-patter of her pulse through his hand on her ribs.

"It's for my sister." Her soft voice was a hot breath on his cheek.

"It's beautiful." His gaze drifted to hers and the streaks of pain he saw there crushed him.

"She was beautiful." Closing her eyes, Gabby shook her head. "I mean, she is still. Wherever she is."

She took a big inhale, and when she opened her eyes, she looked away. Bastien leaned back slightly and shifted so he was sitting next to her, one arm around her shoulder.

"I just wish I knew she was okay." She brushed a strand of hair out of her face. "I haven't changed my number all these years, just in case. But I know she'll never call. Or the call I'll get won't be…"

The rush of blood in his ears made it hard to think, but Bastien knew even with all the time in the world, he'd never know what to say. So he said nothing and just listened. It didn't feel like enough.

"I'm sorry. I didn't mean to be a bummer this early in the morning." She gave him a quick kiss, then shoved his shoulder. "Go to the festival. I'll sleep some more and meet you there later."

Reminding himself that the shove wasn't her pushing him away, he gave her another kiss. This one was longer, lingering, deeper. It took all his strength to drag himself off the couch and out the door. He left for the festival with the taste of her on his lips and the smell of her in his nose. Everything would be great today.

Everything was going wrong.

"Thanks for pitching in." Bastien passed Clementine one end of a long roll of red, white, and blue bunting.

"Of course. It's nice to spend some time just the two of us." The smile on her face helped to smooth away the last of his wearied nerves.

"I wish it was doing something other than fixing my mistakes." He tugged at the bunting a little too hard, and it fell from his sister's hands into the dewy, wet grass. A frustrated huff escaped him, and Clementine clicked her tongue.

"What mistakes?" Clementine looked around at the uneven lines of booths in the town square and shrugged before picking up the end of the bunting. "So you let a seventeen-year-old go a little too far with her ideas about proper crowd flow. It happens. No one will blame you."

Except he would. He wouldn't trade all that time with Gabby for anything, but once he checked his messages from Ashleigh, he realized he should have come by last night to take care of a few things. Or a hundred things. Starting with the complete lack of decorations along the main parade route.

"They'll find a way to blame me one way or another." He grabbed a wayward streamer and wrapped it around his hand before it got tangled in a tree branch. When a car drove by and honked, Bastien raised his hand in greeting. At least he wasn't doing this on his own.

Clementine had answered on the first ring when he'd called her this morning at seven, and she said yes right away to come help. She'd even brought donuts, though they were from the day before. Carl's Café was closed today, one of the only days of the year it was, so that Carl and his dad could run the parade the way the Parsons family had been doing for as long as there'd been one in Jasper Creek.

This was why he loved the Fourth of July Festival more than any other event the town had. There was so much history in it, from the centennial celebrations when the town was little more than a few shacks near a railroad track. Even when Jasper Creek had been a tuberculosis sanatorium, there'd been outdoor events to raise the spirits of the sick who'd come looking for medical help from the Millers.

Without his family, this town would never have survived. It was the least he could do to keep the history going.

He was failing with the cabin, so this festival had to be great. It would also be Gabby's first, and he wanted it to be special for her. Perfect. In the little tidbits he'd heard of her life growing up, it didn't sound like she'd had much. Even events like this had been out of her reach. He made a note to himself to set aside a batch of tickets for kids whose families didn't have enough.

"Are you thinking of Gabby?" Clementine smirked. "You look all dreamy."

"What?" He tugged at his end of the bunting and tied it to a lamppost in front of the entrance to the town square. "No."

"Okay, sure. Keep your secrets for now." Her hands dropped, and the bunting fell briefly before she snapped it back up. "Speaking of secrets..."

When he looked up, a pained look twisted her face. His heart skipped in his chest, and he concentrated on smoothing out the bunting, making sure the red, white, and blue triangles were all perfectly straight.

"I did want to tell you, you know."

Because he was her sister, his Minnie, he knew exactly what she was talking about. He let the uncut edge of the bunting fall to the ground and ran a hand through his hair.

"I just don't know why you didn't. I mean, who better would understand not choosing to be a physician than me?"

She bit her lip. "I'm still in medicine. I felt like you'd be disappointed I wasn't giving it all up like you."

"Disappointed?" He wrapped her in a hug. "Minnie, I could never be disappointed in you. Not even if you started dating pretty boy Austin."

Beneath his arms, she snickered. "Is someone jealous?"

"Yes." It was easier to admit now that he'd told Gabby. He still felt ridiculous about it, his insecurity a tight ball behind his ribs that never seemed to go away.

She shook her head. "Just because you don't have a six-pack anymore—"

"It's not that."

Well, not entirely. Gabby had helped put some of those fears to rest. He was still strong—he knew he was—but he'd never be in shape the way Austin and Jackson were. But that didn't matter, not when Gabby looked at him like he was a treat she couldn't wait to devour.

"I'm jealous because he gets to spend all day with my sister and my dad. And you, before you left for school."

And Gabby, but he didn't say that. Some secrets he would keep from his little sister. Otherwise, what was the point of being an older sibling?

"And you got to spend all that time with Dani and Eli while they were in high school. I barely got any time with you."

"Well, I'm all alone now."

She reached up to plant a kiss on his cheek. "No you're not. Gabby's there."

"For now. She'll move out at the end of the summer."

"Even if you're dating?"

"We're not dating."

Just cooking dinner and watching movies together every night, and eating breakfast together in the morning. And some fun stuff between dinner and breakfast. Not that Minnie needed to know that.

"Well, whatever you are, just talk to her about it." Clementine shrugged, like it was no big deal.

"The last time I talked to someone about our relationship, she left." This got a frown out of his sister. She'd been at college when he'd split with Brenda, and he hadn't really gotten into the gritty details with her or anyone else. Anais had been in med school. Only Jackson knew the full story, but even that had been mostly through text messages in between Jackson's baseball games.

Bastien had gone through it alone, and he wasn't eager to repeat the experience. If Gabby brought it up, he'd talk about it, but he wasn't going to be the one to open Pandora's box and let out something with the potential to destroy everything happy and good in his life right now.

After another hour of work, he walked around the transformed town square.

Despite the chaos things had been when he arrived, Ashleigh had done a pretty good job. A great job, if he ignored the fact that the usual layout was reversed and the ticket booth had been installed at the wrong end of the park.

Walking around with a clipboard, aviator sunglasses, and her ponytail tucked into a hat, Ashleigh looked like a military sergeant preparing for battle. For the first time in he didn't know how long, Bastien could relax and actually enjoy the festival.

When he spotted Gabby walking in near the entrance with Austin, he decided to start now. He grabbed a cup of fresh lemonade from the nearest cart and weaved his way through the crowd to her.

"It's nice to see you." He presented the lemonade to her like it was a bouquet of flowers. "Will you be my partner in the three-legged race later?"

"I hope you know, I plan on winning this year, Bastien." Austin crossed his arms and gave his most furious glare, which, on his perfect face, mostly just made him look constipated. "And Gabby already agreed to be my partner."

"Really?" Bastien's chest squeezed tight.

"Austin, behave yourself." Gabby gave Austin a shove that set off a firework-sized burst of jealousy in Bastien's chest. Unaware of her effect on him, she looked around at the booths and picnic tables. "Of course I'll do it with you. But I thought the parade was first."

"It is." Bastien went through the list of events. The parade included a float contest, which he'd be helping judge, then there were games like tug of war, egg toss, and the all-important sack race. They were supposed to be for kids, but there was always one —very competitive—round for adults.

Clementine walked up just as he was getting to all the different local music groups who'd be playing that day.

"Maybe Clementine will be my partner instead?" Austin flashed her a smile.

"What?" Her face paled and her eyes shot to Bastien, as if looking for help.

Something tense inside his chest smoothed out. Clementine had grown a lot in the past few years, was more independent and knew her own mind. But she was still terribly shy in front of guys. It was one less thing for him to worry about.

"Don't think that will give you any advantage." Bastien waved a finger at him. "Minnie's on my side."

At this, his sister's spine straightened out, and she shook back her hair. "I'd be happy to be your partner, Austin."

Suddenly, Gabby was at Bastien's side, whispering in his ear, "You know, you probably shouldn't race with your toe just finally healed."

He shivered, her words soothing that spot behind his ribs that was still so tense. He hadn't even thought of that. Neither Clementine nor Austin had said anything. The air around him was suddenly brighter, lighter, and his heart lifted like it never had before. Gabby was thinking about his safety in a way nobody else did. Everyone just expected him to hurt himself, but they didn't do anything to make sure it didn't happen again. Warmth spread through him. Gabby cared.

"I can't let him win," Bastien said, heart pounding.

She gave him a funny look, her eyebrows drawn together like she couldn't quite figure out what she was looking at. "It's just a race, Bastien."

She said it so simply, like it was no big deal. He almost believed it.

"Show me around the festival instead. You planned this whole thing, right?" She grabbed his hand and squeezed. "I want to see what you did."

A swell of pride ballooned so fast in his chest he was surprised he didn't pop.

"Okay."

They said goodbye to Austin and Clementine, who were discussing the best strategy to win now that Bastien wouldn't be participating, and walked through the booths set up around the town square.

Everything was running smoothly, however. Ashleigh had managed it all so well there was nothing for Bastien to really help with. A familiar itch of uselessness started to climb up his neck. The only thing keeping him from running off to check if there was enough ice or if the bands had started to arrive was the firm press of Gabby's hand in his.

Luckily, she didn't seem to notice his agitation.

"This is really impressive, Bastien. You do this every year?"

Heat spread across his cheeks and he shrugged. "Yeah. It started as just helping out with the parade the summer after I graduated from college, but then over the years, more and more just fell into my lap."

She raised an eyebrow. "It just fell in, or you asked to do more?"

"Well, no one else volunteered, and this is an important tradition for Jasper Creek. We've had some sort of celebration here since the late 1800s when this was a tuberculosis sanatorium."

"Really? I didn't know that." She leaned toward him and lowered her voice. "Would you tell me more about it?"

If he hadn't already been halfway in love with her, he would have fallen for her then. She was asking him to talk to her about his town's history, and it was like everything in his life had been preparing him for this moment.

As he took her through the history of tuberculosis in Colorado, they continued their slow circuit of the town square. Every so often he'd point in the direction of where a building used to be, and she'd turn her head, a serious, intent look on her face.

"Did you not learn any of this in school?"

"I didn't grow up in Colorado."

"Oh?"

This was the first time they'd gotten even anywhere close to what she'd revealed that night at the Floodline. His heart pounded in his ears. He wanted to know everything about her, but was also afraid to ask too much. The more he knew, the more it would hurt if something went wrong. You could never know everything, and it was the things you didn't know that could hurt you the worst. That's part of why everything with Brenda had been so devastating. He'd known her since high school, so he knew everything about her. At least, he'd thought he had. She'd still left him for something better. Something he couldn't give her.

"I lived in California most of my life until nursing school."

"Austin's from California."

"I know."

Of course she did. Of course she'd already talked to him about it. This jealousy was starting to get annoying, even to Bastien. He couldn't unplug from it, couldn't calm down, couldn't get his heart to stop beating fast at the mere thought of Dr. Gibson.

Gabby had said there was nothing to worry about. Austin had backed off immediately about the race. So why was this still happening?

"Tell me more about Jasper Creek while we wait for the parade to start." Gabby smiled at him, and the battle inside him calmed. His heart rate slowed, and the uncontrollable urge to run away disappeared. She needed him right now, wanted him to talk about his favorite subject. That should be enough.

SEVENTEEN
GABBY

Gabby could listen to Bastien talk all day. Seeing his passion for the town and its history pulled on a string right behind her chest, like her stomach was trying to escape out of her mouth. So she kept it shut. There were too many words she might say by accident. It was safer to just listen.

The only time he was totally silent that morning was while the floats paraded by, his gaze fixed on the clipboard in front of him. He was taking it as seriously as he did everything, and it made her stomach flutter with something very different from the anxiety she was used to.

As soon as the winners for the float contest were announced, he jumped right back into his historical tour of Jasper Creek. They walked side by side, close but not too close, their hands brushing occasionally, sending glittery shivers up her arm.

Would it really be so bad if people know we're together?

She braced herself, waiting for the familiar nasty voice to speak up, to remind her that things would eventually end like they always did, but it was surprisingly quiet today. There was just an overwhelming sense of calm and contentment that sank deeper into her bones the longer Bastien talked.

Then he stopped in the middle of a monologue about logging unions and ran a hand along the back of his neck.

"This must be so boring for you." They were on the edge of the town square, close to the field where the various races and games were happening, and he looked back toward the booths. There were hundreds of people streaming in and out, everyone enjoying the holiday and the beautiful weather. "I should go see if Ashleigh needs help. I'm sorry I got carried away."

"I wouldn't have asked if I wasn't interested." Despite the chance of someone noticing, she reached down and took his hand in hers. "There's something sweet about someone who cares this much about their town."

He blinked down at their joined hands, then back up at her, a smile spreading across his face. "Sweet? I don't think anyone's ever called me that."

"Solid then. Dependable." These were all the things Gabby craved in her life, wrapped in an adorable man who was also her roommate.

He scrunched up his nose and she giggled.

"You make me sound boring."

"What's wrong with boring?" There was that tug in her chest again, the one that told her it was okay to share a little more of herself with him. It was okay to trust him with these tiny pieces of herself. "I work really hard to have a boring life after the childhood I had."

"Where'd you grow up in California?"

She took a deep breath. This was more than a tiny piece.

"I grew up in a lot of different places."

"That doesn't sound boring."

"Exactly." She let herself laugh a little and dropped his hand. They started walking slowly toward the sack races, side by side again, but a little further apart than before. "I tried to keep some things the same for my sister. I would find the closest library so we could spend our weekends there. If there wasn't one, we would go on adventures, exploring the town as much as we could."

It was what she still did now in every new place she landed. Though she'd never gone as far as attend a town festival the way she was today.

"Did you have a favorite place you lived?"

He had that look again, the one that was asking for more. She wanted to give it to him, to tell him she hated everywhere she lived, never let herself like somewhere too much because it was never permanent, because it always got taken away from her. When she opened her mouth to respond, however, a cry from behind them grabbed her attention.

"Help! I think she broke her ankle!"

In an instant, people were running toward the side of the field nearest them. Whatever was happening, Gabby knew it wouldn't be helpful to have so many people crowded around. As she and Bastien hurried over to where the mass of people was gathered, she searched the crowd for any of her colleagues. Jane, Austin, Anais, and Dr. Miller should all be here today, but she didn't see any of them.

In the middle of the throng of people, there was a woman on the ground, clutching her ankle. She looked to be in her early twenties, and it seemed that she'd taken a tumble during the sack race.

"Well, that looks familiar," mumbled Bastien next to her.

Gabby knelt down, told the woman she was an NP, then asked if she could examine her. When she got a short nod in response, she looked up at Bastien. "Can you go find Austin please?"

The woman's face lit up. "Oh yes, Dr. Gibson."

Gabby bit back a laugh at that. Even when in excruciating pain, women couldn't keep their minds off him.

Bastien's face clouded over, but he nodded and stalked off.

All of Gabby's attention was on the young woman, but that niggling, cruel part of her brain was worried about Bastien's reaction. Had she just ruined things with him? Should she have asked him to go find his sister or father instead?

The only reason she thought of Austin first was because he trained in emergency medicine. It made the most sense to get his help, but Bastien might not see it that way.

There wasn't time to worry about any of that, not when the woman's ankle was rapidly swelling to the size of a tennis ball. A deep breath calmed her nervous stomach, and she focused on the patient in front of her.

"Is there a first aid tent nearby?" She looked up into the crowd and was met with shrugs. She let out a huff of frustration when she realized she'd sent away the one person who'd know.

"What happened?" A bright-eyed, ponytailed teenager with a clipboard pushed her way through the crowd. Her face turned a shade of green when she saw Gabby bent over the woman. "Oh no, this is a disaster."

"It's fine. It's just a sprained ankle." Gabby pushed her hair back from her face. "If everyone could just give this woman some space, that would be helpful."

The teen jumped into action, waving her arms importantly. "Step back everyone, step back."

By the time she'd gotten the crowd to disperse, Austin and Bastien were back. Thankfully, Austin was carrying a first aid kit.

She smiled at him. "I think it's just a sprain, but can you check?" Austin crouched down on the other side while Bastien stood, arms crossed, leering at both of them.

"Took a tumble during the sack race, huh?" Austin gave the woman a gentle smile, and she gave a tittering giggle in response.

Gabby looked up at Bastien and made sure he saw her eyes roll at this. The tiniest smile appeared on his face and relief rushed through her.

Maybe she hadn't ruined anything today after all.

"Do you need me to stay?" Gabby asked Austin, who was wrapping the woman's ankle with quick, practiced movements.

"I think I've got this." With one arm, he helped the woman up, letting her lean on him. "I'll just get her to the medical tent."

The crowd dispersed, and Gabby was left alone with Bastien and the teenager, who was babbling a mile a minute about liability and safety briefings before the games.

"It's fine, Ashleigh." Bastien gave her a patient smile. "There's at least one every year. You didn't do anything wrong."

"I'm going to get her some free food tickets."

Bastien shook his head when Ashleigh ran off, chucking softly. "That's what I would have done."

"Looks like this place is in good hands."

"Yeah. Can we go somewhere to talk for a minute?" He took her hand and led her to a storage shed at the edge of the field. When the door was closed and they were totally alone, surrounded by bags full of balls and stacks of cones, he turned and wrapped her in his arms. "Sorry I was so grumpy."

She inhaled his now familiar smell, the heat of their bodies warming her from the inside out. After a few minutes of luxuriating in his embrace, she stepped back. "Did it give you flashbacks to when you hurt yourself at school?"

"More like when I hurt myself in the same sack race a few years ago."

"I thought you were upset I asked you to go get Austin."

He sighed and ran a hand through his hair. "I was."

There was a peculiar twist in her belly to think that someone could like her enough to be jealous. "He really is just a friend. He's a colleague. I would never bring that kind of drama into work."

"I know, and it really has nothing to do with you."

"Oh." It wasn't because of her. A different kind of heat swept across her face, and she took a step away from him, nearly tripping over a loose ball.

"My last girlfriend left me for a doctor."

"Oh." Gabby turned, her stomach tight. "O-oh."

It made more sense now, how even with all her reassurances,

he would still be jealous. Jealous over who she spent her time with. It was still something new for her, and it pleased her more than she knew it should, a squishy, swirly feeling in her chest.

"I know this is a totally different situation, and you're not her, and Austin isn't that guy, but..." Bastien looked down and dribbled a ball for a moment before kicking it into a corner of the shed. "It's hard to let go of the past sometimes."

"I know what you mean." Gabby ran a hand along her ponytail, then took a deep breath. "It's why I move around so much. It's easier for me to just assume I'll have to move than to hope I'll be able to stay."

This wasn't what she'd planned on saying. Bit by bit, it was getting easier to open herself up like this to Bastien. It still sent shivers of panic down her spine, and the nasty voice kept whispering that everything would blow up in her face like it always did. But so far, it hadn't. And that was something.

"You can stay as long as you need, Gabby." He grabbed her hand and squeezed.

"My lease will be up at the end of August. That's plenty of time for me to find something else." Though if that's what she really wanted, then she'd have to start responding to her real estate agent's emails. The thought of leaving the first place she'd ever felt so at home as an adult wasn't an easy thing to think about.

"Well, luckily, I know the landlord, and I think he could be convinced to extend it a little."

He pulled her into his arms with a smile and planted a kiss on her lips that had her head spinning within seconds. The tiny shed was suddenly hotter than the sun shining outside.

Breathless, she drew out of the kiss, and he leaned his forehead against hers. "Would you want to stay longer?" His words whispered across her cheek.

Something in her chest rumbled in warning. It was too soon, too fast. She liked Bastien, was halfway in love with him, but that didn't mean she was ready to live with him permanently. Nothing was permanent in her life except what she could give to herself.

Instead of answering, she tilted her head and kissed him again, this time letting the heat build and the energy between them spark. When they finally pulled away, both breathing hard, she smiled up at him. "Do we really have to talk about this right now?"

He shook his head and swept a few tendrils of hair away from her face with strong, sure hands. "No, there's time."

It was the moment she could have shared it all with him. Her dreams about owning her own home, all the listings she'd been swiping through all week. Except the nasty voice in her head was whispering how it would change things, or worse—make him feel sorry for her.

There was no one with a bigger heart than Bastien, and she was sure that if he knew why she wanted to buy a house, he'd want to help. Refusing his offers was getting harder and harder as time went on. Soon it would be hard to remember how to do anything on her own, and then right when she thought everything was amazing, it would be ripped away.

It happened over and over as a child, in her teens, until finally she turned that part of her off. The same part that was opening up again, not just because of Bastien, but because of Austin and her other colleagues, and the Millers. Because of the people of Jasper Creek.

He kept his hand on hers and led her to the door. "Come on, there's still a lot I need to show you."

Maybe this time real life could shut that voice up for good.

But just in case, she'd keep this part of her story to herself for a bit longer.

EIGHTEEN
BASTIEN

"Should we head to the cabin?"

For the fifth day in a row after sports camps had finished for the morning, Bastien shook his head at Jackson's question.

Another week had passed without any progress on the cabin. As much as he wanted to worry about it, he could say that for the first time in his life, he didn't care what others thought.

"You sure you're okay?" Jackson kicked a soccer ball to Bastien, who put it into the bag at his feet. "There's a lot to do."

"You have a lot to do for the wedding too. I'll talk to my dad about the time limit. I'm sure a few weeks won't really make a difference."

"But then I'll be gone for two weeks, and then you have school starting—"

"Weren't you the one who thought I was doing too much this summer?"

Jackson groaned and ran his hands over his face. "I know. I guess I'm just picking up on some of Anais's stress."

There was a ping in Bastien's chest as he shoved another ball into the bag. "Do you need me to help with anything?"

"No, no, this is on me." He shook his head. "I made the mistake of telling her I liked both roses and sunflowers."

"Amateur." Bastien shook his head. "Don't give her more options. Not with less than a month to go."

"I know, I know." He sighed and started stacking cones. "So now we are spending the afternoon at the florist, trying to incorporate both. If you'd rather go instead of me..."

"I think I'll pass." Bastien's chest filled with light. It shouldn't be that easy to say no, and yet he had. Amazing. "I'll see if Gabby has a break this afternoon."

"How are things going?"

"Good."

That single word didn't even begin to describe how life had been since the Fourth of July. The festival had gone fine with his minimal involvement, and something about that made the pressure to do everything and be everywhere for everyone ease off. Not entirely. But enough that spending his nights with Gabby and lingering over breakfast in the morning with her didn't make his throat thick with guilt and his chest feel like it was caving in.

His chest was certainly feeling something, but it wasn't guilt. It was love. Those early, scary, exciting days of it, and he wanted to revel in it.

Unfortunately, he did have sports camps and she had work, so the kind of lazy summer days he wanted, wrapped in each other's arms, weren't exactly possible.

"Well, I'm glad." Jackson slapped his shoulder, and he hefted the bag full of balls onto his back while Bastien took the cones. The long, uphill walk from the lower athletic fields to the storage shed was just as hard as it had been at the beginning of the summer, and Jackson was clearly slowing his pace for his friend, but Bastien didn't mind. Nothing could bother him these days.

"I take it she's now a permanent resident of your house?"

Well, one thing could bother him. Any time he brought up the offer he'd made at the festival that Gabby could stay longer at the house if she needed, she avoided answering. "I don't know, actually. She doesn't seem to want to talk about it."

"Have you told her you want her to stay?"

"No, but I've told her she can stay if she needs to." He opened the shed, the musty mix of old sports equipment and summer heat hitting his nose.

"That's not the same thing, Bash." They dropped the equipment in the shed, and Bastien rubbed his lower back. It hadn't hurt like this when he'd been in the shed with Gabby, but he'd been focused on other things then.

"Right. So I should just tell her what I want." It sounded simple, so why was he suddenly covered in sweat?

"I know it's been a while since you last dated someone, but people like hearing they're wanted."

Was he even allowed to want her? To want something just for him and not share it with anyone?

He couldn't remember ever feeling like this with Brenda, not in all the years they'd been together. That relationship had been so full of frustration and pain and awkward silences that he'd been ashamed to share the details with anyone, to put that on anyone else. Telling Jackson via text had been safe, kept things at a distance. Needing someone too much was what had pushed Brenda away in the first place.

Now? He looked forward to cooking with Gabby every night. This simple way of taking care of her, of making food that wouldn't hurt her stomach, made him happier than he ever thought possible. She was teaching him so much about cooking. He thought he ate pretty healthily, but since he wasn't training, hadn't been in ten years, things had slipped. The Doritos table for Anais had been a joke because he'd had one at his last birthday.

He was healthier, happier, and full of hope for the future in a way he hadn't been in years.

Was it so bad to want that to never end?

He locked up the storage shed and grinned at Jackson. "Okay, I'll tell her what I want."

Bastien had never been so excited and anxious to go home before. This was what he wanted: to come home and have Gabby be there, and to spend time with her. Of course she'd want to hear that. Jackson was a genius. Today would be amazing.

Bastien walked into the kitchen, sweaty and smelling like grass and mud, but feeling like a million bucks.

Until he saw Gabby sobbing uncontrollably on the couch, and his world fell out from under his feet.

"What's wrong?" Before the words were even out of his mouth, he was next to her, the warmth of her body safe in his arms. Meanwhile, the room shook with the tremors of his inhales. Whatever had happened was bad. And he was sure he wouldn't be able to help. A vise twisted around his heart. He kissed her head, inhaling the salty mix of her tears and the antiseptic they used at the clinic.

She didn't answer right away, but kept crying. Every minute that passed was another painful twist in his chest. It was getting hard for him to breathe, but he kept his inhales slow and smooth. Whatever it was, he wouldn't help if he was upset. He had to stay calm for her.

After what must have been close to twenty minutes, she finally stopped crying. Bastien hadn't even realized it was possible to cry that long. By the end, she was mostly just sniffling into his shirt, mumbling apologies for messing it up that he shushed away, rubbing her arm.

"Tell me what happened."

"My sister called."

Three simple words that were mundane for Bastien, but he knew they were earth-shattering for Gabby. "Oh?"

"She's going into rehab." She didn't sound happy about it.

"That's... good, isn't it?"

"It's wonderful, even if part of me is also furious it took her this long, when the whole reason she stopped talking to me was because I wanted her to go." Gabby wiped at her tear-stained cheeks.

"Families can be complicated."

Her lips tilted up at the same words she'd used with him weeks ago, when he'd been snippy with Anais and didn't want to listen to her advice just because she was his sister. The situation was completely different, but at its core, it was still about the messiness of family. Hopefully, he'd never made Anais cry with conflicted emotion when he finally took her advice way too late, but if he had, then Jackson was sitting there holding her and making her feel better.

"Making it even more complicated is the fact she called because she needs money to go."

Bastien's heart sped up. "And you don't have enough?"

There was so little he could do for her, and it would never be enough. Money was something he had plenty of, and he'd give it all to her if she needed it.

"No, I do."

Cautious hope fluttered in his chest. If she had enough to help her sister, then she didn't need to live with a roommate. This whole time she could have been living on her own, and she'd chosen to accept living with him. Maybe because she wanted him as much as he wanted her?

"So you can help her."

"I want to, so much, I just—" She covered her face with her hands and inhaled sharply. "I'm a horrible person for even saying it."

He rubbed her arm and pulled her closer. "I'd never think that about you."

"It's just something I should have told you sooner."

His stomach took a dip, but he didn't move or change his firm hold on her. Whatever it was, he could handle it.

"I've been looking at houses."

"Oh." Breathing wasn't as easy as it was a moment before, the air thick with the weight of her words. "You mentioned saving up to buy one, but I didn't know you were actually looking. You know you can stay here as long as you—"

"I know, and I'm so grateful, you have no idea."

Gratitude was what he was always looking for, and yet, in this moment, it was the last thing he wanted. He wanted Gabby to stay. He wanted her to want to stay. To want him.

Hot shame washed over him a second later. Here she was crying about her sister, who she hadn't spoken to in years and was going to rehab, while all he cared about was himself.

"I can see why you might have trouble choosing." Again, he'd never been in this exact situation, but he had spent most of his life weighing what he wanted against what he needed to do for others.

"I know you understand." She snuggled, ever so slightly, deeper into his side, and his heart bloomed. Every nerve ending was lit up like the Fourth of July fireworks they'd watched from his —their—porch the other night.

There was a quiet, fizzy moment where they just sat there, breathing, wrapped up together while a new battle raged inside Bastien. The words were on the tip of his tongue, to tell her how he felt, to ask her to stay forever, but he also knew this was absolutely not the right time.

"I think you'd understand more if you knew more." She took a deep breath. "I was homeless for part of my childhood. My dad left my mom right after my sister was born, so I don't even remember him. My mom had her own struggles with addiction, and housing wasn't always stable. Sometimes we lived with friends, sometimes in a car, sometimes in a shelter."

She was looking down at her hands, like she didn't want to look him in the eye.

"Owning a home is something I didn't even let myself dream about until a few years ago. It's like having a house of my own is how I can prove that my past doesn't have to define me."

In a single, breathless moment, all the love he felt for her deepened tenfold. It was like his heart was too big for his chest, too big to keep breathing. She trusted him so much. He didn't know what to say, how to tell her that what she thought was a big deal wasn't for him.

"You're amazing."

They weren't quite the right words, but they seemed to have some impact. The corners of her lips twitched, but she kept her eyes averted.

"I think you'd be amazing no matter how or where you grew up, but I do see now why choosing between helping your sister or buying a house would be hard. She's your past. A house is your future."

Gabby nodded into his chest. "Helping her means she can start over, and I'll have to start over too. It's like I'm still stuck in the past with her."

"That makes sense." Hope, warm and shimmering, flickered at the edges of the room. It was still possible for him to give her what she needed, if she wanted. "You know, I could help—"

"Absolutely not."

The second rejection of the night hit a little harder, and his chest tightened up. She didn't want to stay here. Didn't want him to help.

"Bastien, this isn't your problem to solve. I don't need you to fix this or give me advice. I just need to cry about it, okay?"

It should have been easy. He'd already been doing that, and now she was telling him exactly what she wanted him to do. But he knew it wasn't enough. He knew this was just the first sign of something else. The fear buried itself in his gut, eating away at the happiness from the past few weeks. She didn't need him, not really. Anybody could hold her. If he couldn't fix this for her, then what else was he good for?

"Okay." He rubbed her arm again, and she settled further into his chest with a sigh. She didn't actually cry again, but she sat there, silent, while Bastien's heart raced and his blood pounded in his ears and he wondered what he could do.

If she spent her money on her sister rather than buying a house, and she didn't want his money, then there was only one solution.

He'd finish the cabin and give it to her.

NINETEEN

GABBY

Of course Gabby sent the money to her sister. Did she even have a choice in the matter? It was her sister. She was asking for Gabby's help. Saying no was not an option. After getting more details from the facility in California and guiltily agonizing over it for a week, she slipped an enormous check into an envelope, put a stamp on it, and dropped it in the mailbox.

As she went through the motions at work, a fake smile plastered on her face, the reality of her situation sank in. She was disappointed, but there were more positives than negatives. Her sister was getting the help she'd needed for years. Sure, Gabby would have to save another few years for a house, but she had a place to stay for now.

Except Bastien had been very scarce since he'd come home to find her sobbing on the couch.

As much as she tried not to worry that his early-morning departures and late-night returns were just because of all the work he was doing this summer, part of her knew he was pulling away because of what she'd told him. It was a lot to take in. Maybe he just needed some time to adjust, but it was more likely he didn't want to be with someone who had such a difficult past.

What if her sister needed more rehab later? Gabby couldn't expect Bastien to be saddled with that kind of financial responsibility his entire life. He had his own family to take care of. Gabby would handle things on her own, like she always did. It was just a matter of time before things with Bastien fell apart.

Two weeks before Anais and Jackson's wedding, her real estate agent sent her a listing. Though Gabby had told her the situation had changed, the agent couldn't resist showing her a house at a price that Gabby could still afford with what was left in her now distressingly low savings.

Gabby swiped through the photos during her lunch break, the cozy comfort of the tiny break room more suffocating than it usually was. This house was barely bigger than the room she was in now, which explained the ridiculously low price, but there must be something else wrong with it.

There was only one person she wanted to talk to about this, but her thumb hesitated over the call button on her phone. Her earlier call had gone unanswered, just like all her calls this week had. Bastien always apologized for not responding when he got home, but he was so tired, she hadn't been pressing for details on how he was spending his days.

"You look happy." Austin walked into the break room and greeted her with a smile.

"I am. Or at least, I think I am."

This got the bemused expression from Austin that it deserved.

"I just don't know what to do." She bit her lip.

"About what?"

Without saying anything, she turned the phone around. Austin leaned forward, his eyes flicking back and forth over the details, and nodded slowly.

"Nice house. You going to go see it?"

"I want to, but..."

"You haven't told Bastien about it?"

"This doesn't seem like a text message conversation." She kept chewing on her lip as Austin sat down across from her. "What do I say, 'meet me at the house I want to buy so we won't live together anymore?'"

Even though it might be exactly what he wanted.

Her friend tapped a finger on his lips and lifted a shoulder. "If that's how you want to do it, sure."

Gabby rolled her eyes. "I tried calling, but he didn't pick up. My real estate agent picked up, though, and said she could get me a viewing after work."

"So tell him to meet you there."

Her lip was going to bleed soon with the way she nibbled away at it as guilt clashed with hope. She liked living with Bastien, and she liked him. A lot. Maybe even more than liked him.

But the nasty voice inside Gabby's head hadn't been able to shut up lately. The whole time she'd been sharing about her past, about her sister, the voice had been chanting, then screaming, that it would change things with Bastien. She'd pushed past that, reminding herself that up until now, he'd been nothing but under-standing and supportive.

Faced with days of barely a kiss on the cheek when he came home and went right to bed, ignoring her calls and texts, working all weekend instead of watching movies with her, Gabby had to accept that maybe the voice was right. Things had changed.

"It's okay. I don't want to bother him." Gabby put her phone back into her pocket. "Maybe you could come see the house with me?"

For the first time since she met him, Austin looked surprised. He blinked at her, then licked his lips like he was trying to think of what to say. "Are you sure?"

He may not know everything about her, but she did trust him. "Yes."

The house was perfect. Gabby actually reached out a hand and pinched herself. "Are you seeing this too?" She looked to her left, and Austin was nodding his head. "It looks great. This is an incredible find."

The chances of something coming up with the small amount she now had left after paying for her sister's treatment were infinitesimal. And yet here she was, looking at a house—an entire house, not an apartment—that she had enough money in the bank to make a cash offer on today. Sure, it was less than a thousand square feet and the bathroom looked like it was from the nineteen seventies, but she didn't need a fancy place. Just something that was hers.

The only thing keeping this day from being perfect was that Bastien wasn't with her. It was nice having Austin here, nice to have a friend see the house to make sure she wasn't letting her excitement overwhelm reason, but it wasn't the same.

"So what do you think?" The real estate agent walked over with a big smile. "Will you make an offer?"

Gabby glanced at Austin, who gave her an encouraging nod.

"I think I will." The pride and happiness was like a firework show going off in her chest. She could barely keep herself from jumping up and down.

"There's been a lot of interest, so you'll want to put together your offer quickly, okay?" As the agent went through everything Gabby would need to send in, her heart wouldn't stop pounding.

She needed someone to hold her hand, to hold her, to tell her it would be okay. Austin wasn't that kind of friend.

In the middle of this happy moment, a dark, sticky, familiar kind of fear clung to the edges of her happiness. She wanted Bastien, but did he still want her? That nasty voice that had been getting louder in recent weeks was quick to remind her that this was what always happened.

The agent let her walk around one more time. It was tiny, with a living room with barely enough room for a couch, a kitchen with a half fridge, and the bedroom and bathroom right off the kitchen. It was smaller than Bastien's first floor. The yard was the size of a postage stamp.

But it would all be hers.

The reason for the price other than the size, the agent explained, was because of how close to the road it was. It was also beyond the town line for Jasper Creek, so it wasn't in the same school district.

None of that mattered to Gabby. All she saw was the most remarkable manifestation of her dream.

"I'll send you the paperwork the second I'm home."

Gabby glanced at Austin. "Can you drop me off on your way home?"

"Of course."

The car ride was the most nerve-racking of her life. Her leg bounced a jagged pattern against Austin's car door and she alternated between biting her fingernails to sitting on her hands to stop herself from nibbling them down to the quick.

Austin gave her a worried glance. "Everything okay?"

"Yeah, just scared I'll be too late."

"If you are, there'll be others."

"Not for me."

"It was a nice house, but on the road like that—"

"This is my chance. I won't get another."

He was quiet for a moment as they drove through the outer edge of town. "I get it. This is a big decision. Have you talked to Bastien about it?"

"Why would I? This is my house. My decision to make. All I have with him is a lease. Not a lifetime contract."

Austin raised an eyebrow at that. "Did you have a fight?"

"He'd have to be around for us to fight." She crossed her arms and thumped back against the seat.

They'd been dancing around the topic all week. Austin wasn't an idiot—he could tell how off-kilter Gabby had been—but he seemed to instinctively understand she hadn't been ready to talk about it. Now she was.

"I told him about wanting to buy a house, and he's been scarce ever since."

She didn't share the part about her sister. Now that she'd seen how Bastien reacted to that, she wasn't going to make that mistake again. Even without the added complication of her sister, telling Bastien about wanting to buy a house had clearly been a mistake. He'd told her a few times that she was welcome to keep living with him, and each time she'd avoided answering. Avoiding her was now his answer.

"Maybe he's just busy. There are more camps this week. One of my patients mentioned it when he brought in his daughter with a sprained wrist."

Heat seared her chest. "Well, I should know that. I shouldn't have to guess."

"You're right. But you asked once how well I know him. I know him well enough to know that when he gets focused on something, everything else kind of disappears. He's also terrible at answering his phone when he's like that."

That did unclench something in her, but only a little. Even if she knew she should trust Austin more than the nasty voice in her head, the voice had been with her longer.

No, I don't have to live in the past.

"Thanks, Austin." She gave him a small smile as he pulled up to Bastien's house.

His own smile was a knowing one, and he even added a wink for good measure. "Good luck."

Clearly he wasn't talking about her offer on the house.

That night, she would tell Bastien. He might be upset, but maybe he wouldn't be. Lots of people forgot to answer texts or pick up their phone. It didn't mean anything. And he always apologized for not being available when he got home, didn't he?

When Bastien walked in just a few minutes after Austin drove away, however, his phone was held up to his ear. It sounded like he was talking to someone in his family.

"How many extra chairs do you need?" He gave Gabby a smile and rolled his eyes to the ceiling while he listened to the answer. "I can ask at town hall, but those aren't really meant to be used for private functions."

He plopped down next to her and squeezed her thigh. "I'm sorry," he mouthed. "My mom."

She gave him a smile and shook her head. "It's fine."

It was fine. There were more important things. From the sound of the conversation, the guest list for the wedding had ballooned to an unexpected number, and now they were scrambling to figure out how to make everyone fit.

The call went on for another ten minutes, each second like a screw tightening in her chest. It should have been easy enough. All she had to do was tell him she made an offer on a house. His hand hadn't moved since he sat down, warm and comforting on her thigh. There was no chance that he'd be upset about this news.

There's always a chance.

When he looked at her with another apologetic eye roll, she took that as her cue.

"I'm going to bed," she said softly.

His eyes widened, and he stuck out his lower lip. She kissed his cheek, breathing in his end-of-day mix of sweat and grass and something new tonight. Paint maybe, or varnish. She wanted to ask him about it, if he was working on the cabin again, but there'd be time for that tomorrow. There'd be time to tell him her news as well.

For now, it was enough just to see the pout, to get a shot of dopamine to know that he didn't want her to go to bed yet. His hand tugged for one insistent and reassuring second, before he dropped it to stand up, insisting to his mom that five tables would be enough, he'd used that same amount for a town dinner last year and it had been plenty...

With a sigh, Gabby made her way to her room. Tomorrow. She'd tell him tomorrow, once the offer was accepted.

TWENTY
BASTIEN

"It's done."

Sweat still clung to every inch of his skin, but pride was bursting in his chest. Bastien took a step back and slapped Jackson on the shoulder. It had been a beast of a week, but they'd done it. He'd done it.

"I reckon it is." Jackson wiped his brow and nodded. "You tell your dad yet?"

"I will. I want to talk to Gabby first. Let her know it's hers."

"You sure she wants it?"

It wasn't the first time Jackson had asked him that, but now that Bastien knew Gabby's dream was her own house, and he had the power to give it to her, there was nothing else he'd thought of for the past two weeks.

"I'm sure."

The cabin was done. It had taken so many hours this week he'd barely slept and had barely seen Gabby. When he was focused on a project, he kept his phone off most of the time. He didn't trust himself to answer her texts without giving away his secret, so he kept his replies short.

"What if she wants to keep living with you?" Jackson grabbed the last of the toolboxes from the front porch and walked over to his truck. "I thought that's what you wanted too."

"Of course I want her to. More than anything."

All he wanted to do was curl up next to her and listen to her day, but she'd been just as tired as he was most nights. Then there'd been the almost daily calls from either Anais or his mom, worrying about some new wedding disaster. Two of the smartest, most capable women he knew were letting themselves get worked up over what Bastien knew didn't have to be a big deal. A wedding was a party, like any other. It wasn't the end of the world if the tablecloths didn't match.

It was kind of nice, though, to have them recognize how often he put on large events. The organization and intricacies of timing things right, vendor management, all of it was learned from volunteering, so he'd never thought much about it. To see how incredibly valuable it was, he was even prouder of doing all of that. All he wanted was to be useful to the people he loved, and he finally felt like he was for Anais and his mom.

Everything inside him told him that Gabby would feel the same when he gave her the thing she wanted most. A home of her own.

He hopped into the passenger side of Jackson's truck. "I want her to have the choice. I don't want to make the same mistake as Brenda."

It was perfect, really. This would show Gabby that he wasn't needy. He'd been too pushy before, asking her to stay, telling her she always had a room in his house. Giving her space of her own would let her know that with Bastien, she'd never have to worry about where she'd live ever again.

Jackson turned on the car and headed down the now tidy and mowed driveway. "I don't think that was the mistake you made with Brenda."

This made Bastien pause. "Of course it was." What else could it have been? "I didn't know her that well—"

"No, you didn't."

His friend raised a hand while Bastien tried to keep his anger from boiling over. "From what I saw and everything you told me... I think she was out the second you broke your ankle."

Heart racing, Bastien slapped his palm against the center console. "Exactly. The second I couldn't give her what she wanted. With Gabby, I can do that."

"I thought you wanted to give her the choice to stay or leave?"

"And I thought you were happy for me?" The words came out hot and bitter, which was not how Bastien wanted to be feeling right now.

Jackson pursed his lips and didn't say anything else, which Bastien was grateful for. This wasn't the time to be getting upset. Not when he was feeling so good about this. He'd get some flowers on the way home, hand Gabby the keys, gifting her the dream she'd given up selflessly for her sister, and everything would be great.

Except for the second time in as many weeks, Bastien walked in to find Gabby crying on the couch. In an instant, the flowers tumbled to the floor, and he wrapped himself around her.

Wordlessly, she snuggled into his arms and warmth spread through him. All the work he'd been doing over the past week was so worth it. If he never saw her cry again, it wouldn't be too soon. It was like someone had scooped out his heart from his chest with a rusty and jagged spoon.

"Hey." He planted a kiss on her head.

She sniffed and raised her head, her eyes watery but still that same beautiful rich brown he'd never get tired of seeing. "Hey."

"I know this is probably a stupid question, but is everything okay?"

The corners of her lips lifted, then fell, along with her gaze. "I wanted to talk to you sooner, but you haven't been here."

"I know. I'm sorry. I really wanted to finish the cabin this week."

This seemed to surprise her. She wiped at her eyes and sat up, a frown tugging at her lips. "Why?"

His pulse sped up. This wasn't how he wanted to tell her. There was a plan, involving dinner and flowers and definitely no tears. "Your message said you had exciting news? I came as soon as I could."

She shook her head. "Not exciting anymore."

"Is it your sister?" He squeezed his arms tight around her.

"No, she's doing okay." Gabby shifted, drawing back a little from his embrace. A million possibilities flooded into his mind, scrambling for attention. Her eyes flicked away, landing on the fish tank in the corner. Had he fed them today? He couldn't remember. Gabby licked her lips. "I made an offer on a house. It was rejected. Someone offered twenty percent over asking."

"An offer?" His voice rose in a squeak and he cleared his throat. "Already?"

She bit her lip. "I told you I wanted to buy a house."

"Well, yeah, but then you said helping your sister would mean you didn't have enough."

"There was a one-in-a-million house. It was so cheap because of the location, and it needed work, but I could afford it. In cash." Her lower lip trembled beneath her teeth as a tear fell down her cheek. "But someone had more. Someone always has more. Finding something like that probably won't happen again for years."

The swell of pride was growing bigger in his chest, it felt like he would float away like a hot-air balloon.

"I'm so sorry you didn't get it, but you have a house, Gabby."

She shook her head. "I can't stay here forever, Bastien—"

"No, the cabin." He took her hands in his and brought them to his lips for a kiss. "That's why I've been working on it so hard. I'm giving it to you."

He reached into his back pocket and pulled out a set of keys. A sharp intake of breath lifted her chest high, and she scooted back a few inches on the couch, one hand still in his.

"How much?"

He frowned, the skin between his eyebrows pinching tight. "It's a gift, Gabby."

She threw down his hand and shot up, head shaking and eyes wide. "You can't just give me a house, Bastien."

"Fine, it'll be a dollar or whatever."

"It's not even your house!" A hand went to her forehead, rubbing, while the other rested on her belly, clenching slightly.

It was this sign of her recurring pain that was his first hint that he'd done something wrong. This wasn't just Gabby being coy or wanting more.

He frowned. "I'll talk to my dad. It'll be fine."

"For him to give an employee a house for free?" The hand on her stomach was now rubbing furious circles. Her chest rose and fell with shallow breaths. "Bastien, did you even think about this?"

Now his face heated. "Of course I thought about it. It's all I've been thinking about, all I've been doing, since you told me you wanted a house of your own but thought you couldn't because of your sister."

"You want to save me."

"Of course I do. I love you."

It was the first time he'd ever said those words to her, and he'd practically spat them at her. Disappointment cut him deep across the chest. This wasn't how he'd wanted to tell her. Everything was going wrong.

Her head was shaking. "I never asked for you to save me."

She didn't mention the love part. He didn't know if that was better or worse than actually hearing the words that she didn't love him back.

"I don't want to be given a house. I want to buy a house."

"What's the difference?"

"If you'd grown up the way I did, you'd understand the difference."

He fell back onto the couch. Is that all she thought he saw in her? "That's the past. You don't want that past to define you. You said it yourself."

Her eyes narrowed. "So you do listen to me sometimes."

"I don't see why this is a bad thing." His hands raked through his hair. The panic was rising, clouding his vision and turning the air around him into a sauna. It was all falling apart. Didn't she understand what he wanted to do for her? He stood up and faced her, his hands falling to his sides. "This is for you. It's something you wanted."

"No, what I wanted was for you to come with me to look at the house. But you didn't even pick up your phone. Austin went with me instead."

The name was a punch to his gut. "Of course he did."

"Don't start." She held up a finger, directing it at his face. "I'm sorry your ex was horrible, but if you don't trust me, that's on you, not me. I've done nothing to deserve that."

He knew it was true, and if his brain had been even a bit clearer, he'd have been able to articulate that. Instead, the deep wound he'd carried for years spoke for him, and he was unable to stop it.

"Except look at houses with him, then reject the one I'm offering you."

Her lips pursed tight and her jaw muscles twitched. "You're not offering it to me. This is to make you feel better."

"What? How can you say that? Why would I spend hours on something if it wasn't for someone else?"

"I don't know. I'm a nurse, not a therapist. But I see how you are around your family, around people in this town, Bastien. It's like you'd do anything just for them to pay attention to you. Do you really not feel important to them? To me?" She shook her head.

"Do you really think they need you to run yourself ragged? That I need a freaking *house* to know how you feel about me?"

"How else am I supposed to show I care?" He was fuming now. Saying all the things he'd thought for years, felt for years, and never had the words for before now. "I'm not a doctor like the rest of them. Like Austin. On the Fourth of July, you didn't ask me for help, the coach and former athlete, but him. A twisted ankle doesn't need an emergency room doctor. I wasn't enough for you then, and I never will be for anyone."

The words kept flowing as the tears pooled in her eyes, but he couldn't make himself stop. "I can't save someone's life. I can't name all the bones in the body other than the ones I've broken. I can't do anything in this town other than give my time and energy to it. Millers built this town, and I'm not going to be the one who does nothing for it."

She was standing now, her hair slipping out of her tight pony-tail, tendrils of blond wisping around her face like a halo while her eyes shone bright with unshed tears. "But you don't need to do anything for the town."

"Says someone who's never lived somewhere more than a few months." The instant the words were out of his mouth, he knew they were the wrong ones.

Her face crumpled in on itself like he'd hit her, and the shame spread through him faster than a wildfire in the mountains.

"Gabby, I'm so—"

"Don't." Her eyes were already lined with tears, and she shook her head. "Just go."

Everything inside him was screaming at him to stay, to do something to make this better. To tell her what he really wanted— for her to love him.

Instead, he listened to what she wanted and walked out of the house, crushing the dropped bouquet under his feet as he went.

TWENTY-ONE
GABBY

It took less than an hour for Gabby to get everything packed up and out of Bastien's house.

It would take much longer for the hole in her heart to heal.

"Thanks again for letting me stay with you." Gabby put the last box into Jane's trunk. "And for driving me. I'll work on getting a new car this weekend."

Of course today, of all days, her hunk of junk car had finally died. Everything was falling apart. Everything she thought she was getting this summer had been lost in less than twenty-four hours.

"No problem." Jane closed the trunk with a click and walked to the driver's side door. "Do you know what kind of car you want?"

Gabby shook her head and slid into the passenger seat. "Something cheap."

"Well, let me know if you want me to go with you. My friend works at a dealership in Denver, and I'm sure he could get you a good price."

The simple offer, along with how nice Jane had been since Gabby had called her that morning, was enough to make her want to run from the car and hide from her own stupidity.

Maybe if she'd been more open with her colleagues about her

apartment woes two months ago, none of this would have happened. But if Gabby hadn't come to live with Bastien, she'd never have been brave enough to be that uncomfortable.

It was infuriating, really, that she could appreciate how much she changed while still hating every minute of it and wishing she could forget the past few months of her life.

Her gut situation wasn't exactly in a great spot right now either.

"Gabby?" Jane threw a glance at her, and she realized she hadn't been listening at all.

"Sorry, what?"

"Do you want to stop for some dinner on the way?"

Gabby shook her head. "I'm fine. But we can stop if you're hungry."

"Oh, I should be fine. I had granola and yogurt..."

Gabby let her mind drift off again as Jane launched into a detailed account of everything she'd eaten that morning and what leftovers from last night were in the fridge that they could share. The familiar pattern of her chatter was soothing in an unexpected way. Not having to share about herself was relaxing, a break from the constant pull of vulnerability she'd been dealing with for weeks.

Jane hadn't asked any questions before heartily agreeing to let Gabby stay with her, other than if Gabby was allergic to cats. Jane had three. Gabby hadn't known that until that moment. Maybe she wasn't the only one who kept some parts of her life private.

It took even less time to unpack everything at Jane's cute, two-bedroom apartment overlooking a small lake a few towns away from Jasper Creek. It was the kind of peaceful, planned community where Gabby had always thought she'd end up settling.

Once the final empty box was tucked under the bed, ready to be used again in a few weeks or months, Gabby sat down on the bed. The tears came hot and fast, tracing the well-worn salty lines that were likely permanently etched into her cheeks.

This shouldn't be so hard. I knew it was coming.

Even if this was exactly what she'd predicted would happen, a huge part of her had started to believe it wasn't true. She'd never let herself hope like this, never let herself open up to the possibility of true happiness. Now that she had, it would be impossible to ever build those walls up as high ever again. Pain would be a permanent part of her life again, and she would just have to get used to that.

Like the excellent roommate Gabby knew she'd be, Jane left her alone for most of the evening. At least one thing was easy in this new, painful life. Around seven, Jane knocked on her bedroom door.

"Gabby? Are you hungry? We could go out to eat somewhere if you don't want leftovers."

"Sure." All the saving was pointless. After all, it wasn't like she'd ever get a house. Renting was fine. Plenty of people did that their entire lives. There was nothing wrong with that. It would take some time for Gabby to let go of her dream, but she hadn't had it all that long.

She opened the door to see Jane smiling at her. "I know a really great sushi place not too far away."

"I've never had sushi." Tensing her shoulders, Gabby braced for the barrage of questions. Who hadn't tried sushi? Everyone had. Gabby was tired of feeling so different from everyone, of her life story setting her apart in such an obvious way.

"Really?" Instead of sounding judgmental, however, Jane just sounded curious. "Well, this place is good, but if you don't like it, it's okay."

Gabby breathed out a deep belly breath and her muscles relaxed. "I'll try anything once. It doesn't always go well, but at least I tried."

Like living with someone she had a major crush on and falling for him like it wasn't a sure thing her heart would get broken.

Jane gave her a subtle smile as they walked out the door.

Clearly Austin wasn't her only sharply perceptive colleague, but Jane at least didn't pry.

The drive to the restaurant was full of more typical Jane chatter. This time, Gabby asked more questions, and it was a livelier conversation than they'd ever had before. Jane was easy to talk to, had a lot of interesting stories, and didn't seem to mind that Gabby wasn't as verbose as she was. Maybe Jane was the kind of roommate that could be trusted, relied on. Gabby had never been friends with her roommates before, so maybe she could try it just this once.

Halfway through dinner, Gabby got a call. Her heart dropped into her stomach—already full with delicious sushi—when she saw it was Bastien.

"I should take this outside."

Jane gave her another of her subtle, understanding smiles. Somehow, they'd managed to talk about everything except Bastien tonight, and yet she seemed to understand Gabby perfectly. Maybe Jane had been through something similar. Gabby had never bothered asking, thinking it was too personal, but Jane wouldn't have to answer if she didn't want to.

Out in the warm summer night, Gabby took in the busy parking lot. The restaurant was in a strip mall, with a nail salon on one side and a liquor store on the other. The cars heading in and out of the parking lot were older, used cars the way hers was. It was miles away from the tidy, manicured spaces of Jasper Creek. This was where Gabby belonged.

With a deep breath, she answered the phone.

"Gabby, are you okay?" Bastien said without even a hello.

"Of course I am. Why wouldn't I be?"

"You just left, without saying anything—"

"I left a note. And the last month's rent."

"I don't care about that."

"But I do." This was the problem. "I know money doesn't

matter to you, but it does to me. We had a lease. I am following the terms. I don't want there to be any issues down the line."

"I would never—"

"You don't know that." Gabby let out a breath and the last of her patience. "Bastien, I've been kicked out by church groups, best friends, even family members."

It was almost always because of her sister or mother, never her, but that didn't make it any easier to deal with.

"The past is the past. It doesn't have to define your future. Our future."

"Ask me who I'm staying with."

It was mean, she knew it. Mean and petty and possibly the worst thing she could do to him right now. But if her heart was breaking, then so should his. Let his own past make it impossible for him to move on.

There was a cold silence on the other end of the line.

"Ask me, Bastien." It was heartless, but he'd broken hers so thoroughly she wasn't sure she had one left.

"Who are you staying with?"

"A colleague." With that, she swiped to end the call.

Let him think it's Austin.

If after everything she'd said, after all that time together, if he didn't realize how much she cared about him, then there was no point trying to explain it to him.

TWENTY-TWO
BASTIEN

A colleague.

Bastien didn't need three guesses to know who that must be.

Unfortunately, he'd be seeing that colleague tonight, and he wasn't entirely sure he'd make it through the night without punching Austin in his pompous, perfect face.

For the moment, though, Bastien was alone. The clink of bottles and murmur of chatter was once again the background noise to Bastien's pain, just like it had been all those years ago when Brenda had left him.

Jackson and Eli showed up and slid into the booth.

"Everything okay, Bash?" His best friend raised an eyebrow. "We don't have to do this tonight if you're not feeling up for it."

"Of course I'm up for it. It's your bachelor party." No way was he canceling on Jackson just because he was having a bad night. Or even a bad few nights. It had been three days now since Gabby had moved out, and every day when he got home from sports camp, the house felt too empty. Too quiet, too cold. There were only his dirty sneakers by the door, only his keys on the hook. It felt wrong, but there was nothing he could do about it.

There wasn't even the cabin to distract him. With the work

done and Gabby's rejection of his offer, his dad put it on the market. It would likely sell within a few weeks to some happy, smiling couple from Denver looking for a weekend escape to the mountains.

Austin picked that moment to appear at their table, a pitcher of beer in one hand and a pitcher of soda in the other, which he put down in front of Eli. "Let's get this party started."

That wasn't the only thing Bastien wanted to get started.

"I think you've done enough." Bastien stood and took the pitchers from Austin, the liquid sloshing over his hands and onto the table.

"Hey, watch it." Eli grabbed a stack of napkins and started cleaning up after Bastien.

Good. It was time for someone else in his family to do some work. With a thud, Bastien placed the pitchers on the table. "I may not be a genius, but I think I can manage throwing a party for my best friend."

"Um, okay?" Austin's eyebrows drew together and looked over at Jackson.

"We'll be following my plan tonight, if that's okay with you, pretty boy."

"Actually, since it's my party, we'll be doing whatever I want." Jackson slid out of the booth and stood next to Austin with his arms folded. "And I would like to know why Bastien's being such a grumpy ass tonight."

"Eli's the one with a scowl on his face." Bastien pointed across the booth at the surly teen.

His younger brother stuck his tongue out at him. "You would be too if your brother made this party in public so you couldn't drink."

"You wouldn't be drinking at my house."

Eli rolled his eyes. "Sure."

Normally, Bastien would be teasing, indulging the youngest Miller sibling the way they all did. But tonight he was, just like

Jackson had said, being a grumpy ass, and he had no patience for the kid.

"You know, I think it's past your bedtime. I'm going to call Dad to pick you up." He had his phone in his hand and was swiping to the number when Austin put a hand over his.

"Hey, don't take this out on Eli."

"Don't you start again." In a flash, his finger was in Austin's face and the other man's perfect features had darkened to a beautiful thundercloud. It made Bastien want to punch the guy even more. "I think you've done enough for the people I care about, so if you could just back off, that would be great."

A muscle twitched in Austin's jaw. The rowdy din of the bar was pressing in around them, pushing in from all sides. Bastien inhaled sharply.

"And what have you done lately, other than make them miserable?" Austin's eyes were hard and cold, glinting a threat Bastien had never seen there before.

They both took a step toward each other, Bastien's fists ready at his sides, when Jackson's booming voice carried over the table. "That's enough. Bastien, a word outside?"

"It's fine. I'll go."

Slamming down a pile of bills, he stormed toward the door. He could hear Jackson behind him, people giving him their best wishes as he made his way through the Saturday night crowd. Each congratulations was like a nail in Bastien's chest, sealing shut whatever happiness he'd had at the beginning of the night, leaving only anger and guilt at ruining his friend's party.

Out in the warm summer night, Bastien inhaled and leaned against the building, his gaze taking in the steep stairs that he'd fallen down more times that he could count.

"I'm sorry I'm being such a jerk." The words were out of his mouth before Jackson was even fully out of the bar. "This is your night, and I'm making it about me."

It was the worst sin he could commit, and while guilt was hot in his chest, for once he wasn't hiding it. Not like he had with Anais three months ago in their parents' basement. Now he wanted Jackson to know, wanted everyone to know that sometimes he needed attention too.

"That does seem unlike you." Jackson's steady gaze was familiar and comforting. "Though this mood doesn't. Reminds me of right after the accident."

He didn't have to say which one.

"Or the weeks after Brenda."

"This is nothing like that." He pushed off the wall and started pacing up and down in front of the long, steep staircase he'd drunkenly tripped down as recently as last winter.

"Oh?" Jackson's tone tilted up. "So this isn't about Gabby?"

Bastien remained silent and stared down the stairs, which was all the answer Jackson needed.

"I take it she didn't appreciate your gift."

"She moved out." Bastien rubbed his chest, the pain tight and hot. "I don't know where she is, but I think she's living with Austin. I don't know if she's safe. If she has what she needs."

"If she is with Austin, you know she's safe." Jackson put his hands on his hips. There was a burst of laughter and clinking glasses as the door to the bar opened behind him. Carter Hayes poked his head out and raised his eyebrows, but Jackson waved him back inside. "And I think she's capable enough to get what she needs on her own."

"I know." This was the truly painful part. "She doesn't need me. Just like—"

"I thought this was nothing like Brenda?" Jackson raised an eyebrow. "And I'd agree. You were never happy with her the way you are with Gabby."

"The way I was."

"The way you will be again once you figure out what to do."

"How did you fix it?" Bastien turned to him, the endless drop of the staircase and its reminder of all his past failures behind him now. "With Anais? You did something like this at one point."

"Uh, I never gave her a free house she didn't ask for." The humor at the edges of Jackson's lips was hard to miss. He rubbed his chin and gave a slight nod. "But I know what you mean."

Hearing it out loud, it did sound ridiculous. Bastien had given someone a house. Someone perfectly capable of managing her own life, of saving and buying it on her own. Someone to who buying it would signify a huge milestone considering what she'd been through.

"Oh no." Bastien put his hands over his face and leaned against the wall, wishing he could sink into it and disappear. "I really messed up."

Jackson's hand landed on his shoulder, just slightly harder than it needed to be. "Oh yeah."

"No helpful suggestions?" Bastien dropped his hands to glare at Jackson, who shrugged in the most nonchalant and unhelpful way possible.

"All I did was talk to Anais. Told her all the things I hadn't before so she'd understand."

"I don't know if that'll really help in this situation." Bastien shook his head. "We talk—talked—all the time." His chest tightened at the need to use the past tense. "What could I say to justify what I did that I haven't already said?"

"Maybe the truth? That you weren't thinking about her, you were thinking about you." Jackson perched next to him against the wall.

Bastien's heart dove into his stomach. The ultimate sin. The unforgivable one. He pushed off the wall and made his way to the top of the stairs. "That's what Gabby said I was doing too."

"Bash, you spend ninety-nine percent of your life taking care of others. Even before you got hurt, it's just who you are, who you've always been. It's okay to sometimes think about what you want."

In the distance, a car door slammed in the parking lot. The

laughter from a group of friends made its way up the stairs, and Bastien stepped out of the way to let them pass into the bar.

"I always seem to do it at the worst times. Like tonight."

Jackson waved that away. "If I wanted a big party, you know I could have done it myself. Some of my former teammates were talking about going to Vegas. I opted to do something small."

"None of them are coming to the wedding?" Heart in his throat, he turned back, expecting to see Jackson looking disappointed, but there was no trace of it in his face.

"A few. Madison and Danielle are excited about that."

The mention of Jackson's younger sister sparked something in Bastien. All of Jackson's career, he'd been working toward making enough money to get Madison out from under their parents' control so she could make her own choices. He hadn't made any decisions for her, but given her the possibility. That's what Bastien thought he'd been doing too. But Gabby could do all that for herself.

"The only reason I offered Gabby the cabin was because she'd spent her savings to help her sister." He didn't give further details, since that was Gabby's private life, but he could trust Jackson with this surface-level comparison.

"That was her choice to make, Bash." There was a slight shift in Jackson's face, a tightening of his lips and around his eyes.

"I know, I know." Bastien ran his hands through his hair, pacing again in front of the bar, keeping clear of the stairs. "But I had the solution for her. She needed a house, and I had one. What's the problem?"

Jackson leaned against the building and took a sip from his glass. The sun was setting behind the trees, and the entire bar was bathed in a pink light. The air was warm, and a gentle breeze whispered between them. It should have been the perfect night to celebrate with Jackson, and Bastien was ruining it.

"You've only ever offered me money once, Bash, and I said no. You let it drop, no problems. Why is Gabby different?"

The answer came to him instantly, but he pushed it away. Hot embarrassment spread across his chest, burning away everything else he was feeling. "Do I really have to say it?"

"I reckon I know what it is, but I might be wrong." Jackson shot him a smug grin.

Bastien inhaled, then let the words flow out of him, a jumble of sounds. "I knew you'd be fine. You didn't really need me to help, and I knew we'd still be friends. But if she doesn't need me to help her... then she won't want me around anymore."

Jackson frowned. "Looks like I was wrong. Brenda really did a number on you, didn't she?"

Pressure built behind Bastien's eyes, his throat thick with the words he didn't want to say out loud. Swallowing them down, he turned away and watched the last rays of the sun filter between the trees. "I wasn't important enough for her. She didn't need me to get the life she wanted. She found someone else who could give that to her. To give her what she needed."

"What she wanted." Jackson rolled his eyes. "You've only known me as a poor student and minor league player, but remember, I grew up rich. Nobody needs that kind of money. They want it, then they want more. What they need is to feel safe. And heard. And seen."

"Gabby makes me feel like that."

"You probably made her feel like that, too, until you ignored what she was saying and thought you knew best."

Bastien scrunched up his face. "I do that a lot, don't I?"

"Well, you did make my party here and not Vegas, so you're not totally hopeless." With a chuckle, Jackson put a hand on his shoulder. "There's a fine line between caring and smothering. Helping and hovering."

"I know." He did, but it was too late for it to change anything with Gabby. "I don't think it makes a difference now though."

"I reckon you'll think of something before too long."

"You certainly have a high opinion of me."

"Why wouldn't I?" Jackson tilted his head, brow furrowed. "C'mon, let's get back inside. Matt Hayes promised me a free pint to celebrate, and I'm not about to waste that because you're being a grumpy ass."

Bastien laughed and followed Jackson back inside.

When they got back to their booth, Clementine had taken Bastien's place and was laughing at something Eli was saying. Austin had a wide grin on his face like he was having the time of his life.

"Looks like the party started without me."

"Oh, I can go." Clementine stood up. "I know this is guys' night. I just wanted to tell Eli what happened in class this week."

She looked so happy, Bastien's chest gave a knowing tug. Maybe some part of him *had* been upset that she'd stayed in medicine instead of following his path. It had been nice to think that she was still his mini me when it felt like everyone else had left him behind.

That wasn't fair, and he knew it. Just like he knew he'd gone too far by offering the cabin to Gabby. Unlike his family, who he knew would love him no matter what, Gabby could and should walk away if he wasn't the right one for her.

Clementine stood up and gave her brother a quick kiss on the cheek before he slid into the booth. She waved at the four of them.

"Have fun tonight."

"We plan on it," Jackson said.

Matt had just appeared in the distance with a tray full of ice cream.

It was one thing to be selfish sometimes about what he wanted, but tonight wasn't about him. Just like Jackson would always be there for him, Bastien would be there for the ones he loved. Even if they didn't love him back.

TWENTY-THREE

GABBY

Living with Jane meant a week of living by someone else's schedule. Without her own car, Gabby relied on her colleague to get her to and from work. On the nights the clinic was open late, Austin drove her home. The lack of autonomy should have made Gabby's skin crawl, but with her heart still bruised and her insides raw, it was nice to let others take care of things.

This would have been impossible to imagine at the beginning of the summer. Thinking about her time with Bastien, how much he'd changed her for the better, was still painful. The lack of him was a wound, open and festering, but invisible to anyone else.

Well, not quite invisible. Jane and Austin knew something was up and were treating her with kid gloves. They avoided bringing up his name or asking what Gabby's plans were for the fall.

The early-morning stops at Carl's Café with Jane were a welcome escape from the hovering, and a nice change from granola bars alone in her room. Even if Gabby's stomach wasn't super happy about it, Jane's chatter over breakfast at the café was usually an entertaining distraction.

Today, it was a discussion of the show they'd watched together the night before. Surprisingly, Jane liked sci-fi comedy as well, though Gabby hadn't asked if she'd seen *Serenity*. That was still too attached to Bastien in her mind.

"Mind if I join you?" Austin appeared at their table.

"And me?" From behind Austin, Hunter peeked his head around.

"Is this another surprise party for me? I can't take any more." Now Anais was there too. After a minute of shuffling around the table and adding more chairs, the staff of Miller Family Medical, minus Dr. Miller, were all sipping from their mugs and chatting about—what else?—the wedding.

Gabby waited for the anxiety to bubble up in her belly, for her stomach walls to clench with fear, but she was surprised to find she was looking forward to sitting with everyone. There was something comforting about being with colleagues outside of work in a social setting that had less pressure than the parties at the Millers' house.

"One week to go, Anais!" Hunter grinned. "How are you feeling?"

"Fine." Anais gave them all a smile that didn't quite reach her eyes. "A lot to do."

She was working until Wednesday, then would be off for two weeks. If it wouldn't have been so incredibly inconvenient for everyone—and the fact that she'd miss them all terribly—Gabby had seriously considered quitting. Then she wouldn't be expected to go to the wedding.

"Anything we can help with?" Seated next to Anais, Austin put a hand on her shoulder and she leaned into him slightly.

"It'll be fine. I just want to be married. I don't want a wedding."

Gabby's chest caved in from empathy. It was such a vulnerable thing to say, like she was witnessing something private, personal, that you had no involvement in. The fact that Anais felt comfortable enough to say something in public, where anyone could hear, in front of her colleagues, was something Gabby could never imagine doing.

"It's a little late for that." Austin chuckled softly. "But if you want to drive off to Vegas tonight, I won't tell anyone."

"Don't tempt me." Anais looked around, and her eyes widened like she'd just remembered she was in Carl's Café instead of the break room at the clinic. Curious eyes glanced over at their crowded little table. Clearly wanting to turn the conversation away from the wedding, Anais turned to Gabby. "How are you doing, Gabby?"

There were at least a dozen ways she could answer that. Which one was Anais looking for?

"I'm okay."

"Really?"

Gabby's stomach dipped, her throat tight. "Yeah."

Austin was giving her a look that was halfway between exasperated and sympathetic. What did he expect her to do, bare her soul in Carl's Café like Anais had? The weight of a dozen pairs of eyes on their table was heavy on her shoulders, but the others didn't seem to notice. There was a slight churn in her stomach, a warning that if she didn't start breathing deeper, a full-blown episode would be upon her. Gabby grabbed her glass of water and downed it.

"I do hope you'll still come to the wedding. There'll be a ton of people there." At this, Anais let out a heavy sigh and lowered her voice. "Too many, really. It'll be easy to hide in the crowd."

Gabby shot an angry glance at Austin, but her stomach dropped when he just shrugged and shook his head. Had Bastien said something to his sister? Or was Gabby's pain that transparent? At least she wouldn't have to quit. If Anais didn't expect her to be there, then not showing up was apparently an acceptable option.

"Oh, um, yeah, I may have a conflict that just came up." Gabby hunted in her brain for an excuse, any excuse that seemed halfway plausible. "My sister asked me to visit."

It was a lie, and now Austin glowered at her. Gabby's belly clenched at just how untrue it was. There'd been no follow-up from her sister, not even a phone call to thank her for sending the money. The check had been cashed, so at least Gabby could be sure her sister was getting the care she needed. That's all that mattered.

"Well, if you do end up being able to make it, I'd be thrilled to have you there." Anais turned to Austin now and stuck a finger in his chest. "And if you could avoid fighting with Bastien, that would be great."

"Fight? When did you fight?" Gabby's heart sped up.

Hunter and Jane leaned in, eager to hear as well.

"It's nothing." Austin glared at Anais, then raised his voice a little to be sure everyone around them heard his answer. "Just typical trash talk between guys at a bachelor party."

"Hmm, that's what Jackson said." Anais narrowed her eyes and sat back in her chair. "You sure it won't mess up anything this weekend?"

"Of course not." Austin smoothed a hand up and down Anais's arm. "You know neither of us would do that to you on your big day."

"Ugh, please don't call it that." She let her head fall into her hands with a dramatic sigh. Jane and Hunter tittered.

"Fine, the most miserable day of your life."

Gabby held back a laugh, and Anais let out a chuckle.

"As long as I have everyone there I care about, I won't be miserable." She glanced over at Gabby, then let her eyes drift to Jane and Hunter. "That includes everyone at this table. You've helped so much this summer, you have no idea."

There was a jumble of voices all saying different things. "Don't mention it," "Of course, sweetie," "Happy to help," but Gabby remained silent. Everyone around the table had helped her this summer, and they didn't even know it. She took a deep breath.

"I want to thank all of you as well." Four heads turned to look at her, and her pulse tripped. Fighting against her growing nausea, she kept going, keeping her eyes on her plate. "I know I'm not the most outgoing person and I don't like to share a lot—"

"Don't worry, I share enough for everyone combined," quipped Jane, and everyone chuckled.

Gabby let her lips turn up. "You've welcomed me and been so nice, even given me a place to stay, but haven't pried." Her eyes slid to Austin's and caught his smirk. "Well, most of you haven't pried. I just want you all to know how much it means to me. I haven't always felt safe, and learning to trust this feeling is new to me. So thank you for being patient with me."

Hunter reached out a hand and laid it on top of hers. "I think that's the most I've ever heard you say that wasn't about a patient."

They all laughed, Gabby included, then she shook her head. "I don't think it'll be a regular occurrence. That was scary as hell."

"We're doctors. We know not everyone with the same illness needs the same kind of treatment, or will present the same kinds of symptoms." Anais smiled, kindness shining through familiar green eyes.

Jane was next to her and put her arm around Gabby's shoulder to give her a hug. "We all know you're quiet. That's why it was so nice to see you get together with Bastien. He could use a little calming down sometimes."

Her head shot up. "Wait, you all knew we were together?"

They were all giving her the same "are you kidding me?" look.

"That boy never even brought his sister or father lunch, but he was there every day last week for you." Jane raised an eyebrow. "That's not something roommates do."

The heat rose quickly in Gabby's face, and she took a long drink of water while she thought about how to respond. Even after draining her glass, her throat was dry, but she had to ask the most important question.

"Anais, you don't think your dad—"

She held up her hand. "He has no idea. Still just thinks you were roommates."

The past tense cut into Gabby's fragile happiness like a broken piece of glass. She wasn't sure it would ever stop hurting.

"Though he probably would have figured something out if you showed up to the wedding together..." Anais's voice raised hopefully.

Gabby shifted in her seat, four pairs of eyes on her. "I'm sorry. I just don't think I'll be able to make it."

"Well, if your schedule opens up, you're welcome to join us. It won't be the same without you."

From beneath the table, she felt the reassuring pressure of Austin's foot on top of hers. He gave her a small smile, no hint of his usual smugness.

She wanted to go, to be with her friends, to celebrate Anais. But she wasn't sure her heart could handle it.

"Thanks. I'll think about it."

***

BASTIEN

Bastien was in the middle of his third rewatch of *Serenity* that week when Anais burst in his front door.

"Bibi, I need you." There were five different sizes of boxes stacked in her arms, and he could see more out on the porch.

He stayed where he was. "I'm busy."

Anais stopped in the middle of the room, her eyebrows drawn together tightly in a single straight line of sisterly concern.

"Are you sick? You can't be sick at my wedding."

"I can do whatever I want." Which, for the past week, had meant sitting here doing nothing at the end of the day. With the lack of brilliant ideas on how to fix things with Gabby, he'd descended into a funk that not even promises of free pints at the Floodline from Jackson had moved him off the couch.

Gently and slowly, like he was a wild animal about to attack,

Anais put her box on the floor. Then she closed the door and sat down next to him on the couch.

"Bastien, what's going on?"

He turned up the volume of his movie.

She grabbed the remote and clicked off the TV. "Bastien, stop being such a brat."

"Oh, I'm the brat now? For wanting just one evening to myself to do what I want?"

Now her lower lip started to tremble, and Bastien knew with a guilty tug of his gut he'd gone too far. "I thought you said you'd help if I needed it?"

If there was one thing he couldn't handle, it was his sister crying. In an instant, his arms were wrapped around her. "I'm sorry, of course I'll help. I don't know why I just did that."

She sniffed into his shoulder.

"I think because you know I still love you, even if you're in a bad mood." She sat up and wiped her eyes.

Bastien was getting very tired of people he cared about doing that on this couch.

"You'd be the only one." He leaned back and rubbed his hands over his face.

"You know that's not true."

"Fine, the whole family." He grunted, thinking of his conversation outside the bar this weekend. "Jackson too."

"I think Gabby could handle these moods if you let her."

His eyes shot to hers, and anger zipped through him. "I thought you were the one who needed help."

"Right." She flipped her hair over her shoulder and took out a box full of personalized cork wine stoppers. "I need to make two hundred favors tonight."

"You said you weren't doing favors."

"Three weeks ago, I also wasn't having a sit-down dinner, and yet you found me eight tables and a tent for that very purpose."

He shook his head. "You probably should have just gone to Vegas."

Her lips turned up. "Probably."

They worked in silence for a few minutes, putting the wine stoppers into little pieces of cardboard, then carefully inking in a name and table number based on a printed list. When Bastien got to Gabby's name, his hand stilled. Anais peered over at the list and bit her lip.

"I don't think she's coming to the wedding."

"What? Why not?" His heart stopped.

Anais shrugged, her eyes on her work and slipped another cork into its cardboard holder. "It'll be too awkward for her."

"She said that?"

"No, she didn't have to. She would barely look at me at work this week. She's always been shy, but this is even more withdrawn. Living with Jane must be hard for her."

His heart stopped, his hand frozen over a pile of wine stoppers. "I thought she was living with Austin."

Anais laughed. "Who told you that?"

"She said she was living with a colleague."

"And you assumed that meant Austin?"

"Well, he didn't deny it the other night..."

She whirled on him, eyes flashing. "Is that what your fight at the Floodline was about? Both he and Jackson refused to tell me."

Somehow, that made him hate Austin just a tiny bit less.

But only a tiny bit.

"It wasn't a fight. I just wasn't fawning all over him the way he's used to."

Anais clicked her tongue. "You're worse than Jackson. Who got over his jealousy in about three seconds, by the way."

"Well, good for him. Professional athletes can afford to do that. Not teachers."

Anais threw up her hands. "Bastien, when are you going to get over what happened ten years ago and realize how amazing you are?"

His heart stopped. "You really think that?"

She'd never said that to him. No one in his family had.

Gabby had though. A few times. He'd even started to believe it, until she left. If he was amazing, then why would she leave?

Maybe because you're an idiot who gave her a house she didn't ask for?

Oh, right.

"Of course I think that." The exasperation on his sister's face was at a level he hadn't seen since they were ten and he'd asked if because they were twins he'd grow boobs too. "You do so much for this family, for the town. You were always generous, but it was like your accident kicked it into overdrive. Now you do everything."

He crushed a cork in his hand. "Except carry on the Miller tradition."

"You mean our tradition of taking care of people? You're telling me you don't do that?" She plucked the destroyed favor from his fist and gave him a new one.

"Not like you do."

She inked another name in her precise, careful handwriting. "Anyone can do what I do. You could have, too, if you weren't so talented with a soccer ball."

"I was talented."

"Stop it." The pen dropped from her hand. "I've seen you coach. I've seen your teams. No other town our size has made it to state championships."

Heat was pooling in his face. Bastien concentrated on the pen in his hand and wrote a few more names on little pieces of cardboard before he could find words again.

"Thanks for saying all this." He slipped another finished favor into the box. "It's nice to hear sometimes."

He looked up, and her gaze had softened. "I'm sorry we don't tell you more. It's easy to take you for granted sometimes. I just know you'll always be there. It's the only way I managed to leave home for so long for school. I knew you'd be here taking care of everyone."

Pride swelled in his chest. She hadn't relied on their mom or dad. Because she knew she had Bastien.

Anais wrapped her arms around him. "Thank you."

He hadn't realized how much he needed to hear those two words from his sister's mouth until they were there, floating in the air between them as they hugged. Everything hot and angry in Bastien calmed, the cooling effect of two little words like a balm on an itch he'd been scratching for years.

He swallowed hard. "So what should I do about Gabby?"

"Oh, I have no idea." Anais pulled out of the hug and shrugged her shoulders. "I'm getting married in four days, Bastien. I have other things to worry about."

He gave her a gentle shove, then started working on the favors again. "Like you couldn't do both at once if you didn't want to."

"Do you want me to fix this for you?" Raising an eyebrow, Anais threw another wine stopper into the box. "You want me to get involved, boss you around, tell you exactly what to do?"

"Well, when you put it that way..." Bastien ran his thumb along the rough cork on the top of the wine stopper and bit his lip. "Can I get a hint at least?"

Anais inhaled slowly then crossed her arms. "Why exactly did you offer her the cabin?"

How did she know about that? Oh, right. Jackson.

"She needed it." He shook his head, his hands busy with making favors, helping Anais, doing what came so naturally he didn't know how he kept getting it wrong. "No, she didn't. I wanted to give it to her. I wanted to be the one to solve all her problems."

"I think she does a pretty good job solving them on her own." Anais leaned back on the couch, her eyes laser focused on him. "What did you really want?"

A wine stopper rolled to the edge of the coffee table where they were working, but he did nothing to stop it falling to the ground. He considered lying to his sister, but there was no reason to. And she'd see through the lie anyway. "To show her I love her."

Anais's eyebrows shot up. "Is that what this is?"

There was an ache, deep inside, a Gabby-shaped hole that he wasn't sure would ever be filled. In comparison, Brenda had barely left a sliver, which had closed up at some point this summer without him even noticing. "What else would it be? She's the only one who lets me be just me. She doesn't expect anything from me. What do you give someone like that?"

Anais laid a hand on his shoulder. "You don't need to give her anything other than your love and attention. You're enough, Bastien, without doing anything special."

For the first time in a long time, he believed it. But how could he show Gabby she was more than enough for him?

TWENTY-FOUR
GABBY

Once again, Gabby found herself checking her outfit before walking into the Millers' house. Technically, she was walking into their backyard. An elaborate arch of flowers stretched across the same opening in the fence she'd walked through for the Easter picnic just a few months ago.

The yard was full of bright dresses and smiling faces. The sound of laughter and chatter floated over the gentle melody of a string quartet. For the moment, no one had noticed her enter, but that didn't stop her heart from pounding or her legs from shaking.

This is a bad idea. I should go.

As she turned to walk right back out, her heel sank into the ground and she froze in place, unable to move.

In the midst of the chattering crowd, no one seemed to notice Gabby and her predicament. While there were some familiar faces, there was no one she felt comfortable enough calling attention to herself and the help she needed.

I wish Bastien were here.

The traitorous thought had been popping up more and more over the past week.

After standing in the same spot for several minutes, sweat

collecting in the dip of her chest and soaking the back of her dress, help finally appeared in the form of Austin. He looked exceptionally dapper in a light gray linen suit and no tie, the top button of his shirt left open.

"You came." He looked thrilled, though the women in the crowd around them looked the opposite.

"I'm stuck here."

"If it's too hard, I can cover for you while you sneak out."

"No, my heel is stuck in the grass."

His eyes lit up with understanding—and laughter that he was too nice to let out. "Allow me to be of service, milady."

With an exaggerated bow, he bent down and grabbed the back of her calf while she put a hand on his shoulder to balance herself.

A single sharp tug was all it took to liberate her foot, and she let out a relieved breath. "Thank you."

"No prob—" Austin stood up and his face went blank.

"It's my sister's wedding day, Gibson," said a voice behind Gabby, and her heart almost stopped. "So I won't make a scene. But I'd appreciate it if you made yourself scarce."

With a familiar smirk and mini salute, Austin scampered off into the crowd, much to the delighted excitement of the single women in attendance.

Gabby's attention was entirely focused on the man behind her. With shallow, short inhales, she turned slowly, careful not to let her heel sink back down again.

The intense, green eyes of Bastien Miller were fixed on her.

"I won't apologize for wanting you all to myself, Gabby." His words were a low rumble that started in the base of her spine and shivered up her back. "I've always shared everything I can with the world. My time, my energy, my attention. But I don't want to share you."

The world tilted under her feet, and she had to grab on to him, or risk falling onto the grass. His arms wrapped around her, holding her up, holding tight to her like he was never going to let go.

What could she possibly say to that?

"Hello to you too."

His lips curved up in as private a smile as was possible in a crowd of several hundred.

"Let's go somewhere to talk?" he asked, his lips close enough to her face she could feel his breath on her neck.

"Don't you have to help with the wedding?"

"They'll be fine."

He slipped his hands off her, wrapped one hand over hers, and tugged her around the side of the house and through a door. Whether people noticed them or not, Gabby couldn't say. Her eyes were only on Bastien.

The brightness of the day was doused when they walked into a finished basement. It was bigger than most of the apartments she'd lived in. Three walls were lined with overflowing bookcases. On the fourth was a wine rack stacked all the way to the ceiling, full of dusty bottles that probably cost more than the house she'd made an offer on.

The doubt creeping in was swirling away in her already anxious gut, but Gabby took a deep breath and focused on the warmth of Bastien's hand in hers. His words reverberated along her spine.

I don't want to share you.

He spun her around, trapping her against the wall by putting his hands on either side of her head.

"Hi." Her voice was small and wavering, her breath coming in short, sharp bursts.

"Hi." His smile was slow and hypnotic.

Just tell him.

Ever since breakfast with her colleagues, she'd been thinking about how rarely she had truly shared with Bastien how she felt. Yes, she'd shared parts of her past, and she'd let herself cry in his arms. It was entirely possible she hadn't shown that she cared about him in a way he understood.

The offer of the cabin had been his way of showing he cared about her. More than anyone ever had. There were his strong words, as well.

And the way he was looking at her.

"I'm sorry," she said and bit her lip to keep it from trembling.

A line appeared between his pinched eyebrows. "What do you have to be sorry for? I'm the one who messed up. I'm sorry, Gabby, so sorry."

She brought her hand up to brush his cheek. "You wanted to take care of me and—"

"No." He shook his head. "I was trying to do what I've always done. Solve someone's problems, give them whatever they need so that I could feel needed. I don't want to do that with you."

"Oh?" She found that very hard to believe, given how his hands were pressing into her back and his eyes were fixed on her lips like a drowning man reaching for the side of a boat.

"I mean, I don't need to do that with you. I've never had to give you anything other than my time and attention. You've never made me feel like I wasn't enough, just the way I am."

Warmth spread through her, and she leaned forward to place a gentle kiss on his cheek, lingering over the smell of summer clinging to his skin. "You are enough."

"So are you. I love you, Gabby." He took a deep, shuddering breath.

"All you ever had to do was say it. I don't need you to show me. I can feel it." Gabby leaned her head against his and closed her eyes. "I love you too, Bastien. I'm sorry I didn't say it sooner. Then maybe you wouldn't have felt like you needed to do something so…"

"Ridiculous?"

She could feel the laugh in his words against her cheek.

"So generous." She kissed him then, letting their lips slide together and letting herself fall into it, into him, completely.

They probably would have stayed like that all day, missing the wedding entirely, if Clementine hadn't come looking for Bastien. In their little bubble, everything felt so perfect and wonderful that Gabby wasn't sure it would hold up in the light of day. They'd apologized, explained the best they could, but had anything really changed?

Gabby got her answer halfway through dinner. She was seated at a table with Austin, Jane, and Hunter, laughing and enjoying the food, when Bastien appeared at her side.

"Would you come sit with me?"

Her hand dropped the fork she was holding. "With your family?"

"I want you next to me."

Well, that was clear enough. No more little private bubble. Gabby inhaled slowly, her nerves zinging with uncertainty.

"Or I can sit here, if you want." He looked around at her colleagues. "Wherever you're more comfortable."

She caught Austin's eye, but his expression was unexpectedly blank. Jane and Hunter, however, had no such restraint. They were grinning like she'd won the lottery.

"I would be more comfortable here." The Miller family's table was at the front of the tent, with all the other tables facing it. Just the thought of having so many eyes on her was enough to make the food she had been able to eat threaten to reappear. "But I don't want to take you away from your family. Everyone will expect you to be up there with them."

"They'll be fine without me. I don't care what anyone here thinks. I want to be next to you."

A slow, sparkling joy started in the pit of her stomach and flowed through her. He could have offered her a hundred houses, and none of it would have meant as much as this. Finally, he could say what he wanted, and it didn't matter what his family or the town wanted from him.

She took his hand and beamed up at him. "Then stay."

Austin gallantly offered his chair, a rueful smile on his face, then wandered off toward the front table as Bastien sat down.

"Will you stay? With me?" Bastien's voice was low, too quiet for Jane or Hunter to hear.

She squeezed his hand. "I will."

There was no guarantee things wouldn't change, that this new, happy life she'd built for herself wouldn't end unexpectedly. But she knew she would no longer be alone if it did, and that made all the difference.

EPILOGUE

It was the last family game night of the year, and Bastien had an announcement to make.

He and Gabby had gotten married.

In Vegas.

Three days ago.

"Are you sure you're okay with telling everyone?" He slid his hand into Gabby's as they crunched their way up the snow-covered path to the front door of his parents' house. "We can keep it to ourselves a little longer."

"It's fine." She squeezed his hand, then shivered a little in the freezing, late-December air. "I know you're just dying to see the expression on your sister's face."

He smiled, and a particular kind of warmth spread through him, the kind that you only felt when you'd truly one-upped your siblings. "It will be nice to see her speechless for once."

"You're sure they won't be mad?" There was a trace of fear in her voice, and he pulled her to face him, a few feet away from the door. She bit her lip and looked down. "We've been together less than six months. They barely know me."

"What do you mean? You work with two of them every day,

and we're here for meals at least twice a week." He cupped her cheeks with his gloved hands and tilted her head up so he could look her in the eyes. "Besides, not everything takes forever to become permanent."

The kiss he planted on her lips was soft and warm.

"Plus this way we'll get the tax benefit for this year."

She laughed, which had been his goal. "Yes, that was top of my mind when I proposed last week."

The day after Christmas, just the two of them together at home, watching *Serenity* for probably the hundredth time, she'd snuggled close to him and said, almost in a whisper, "I never thought I'd feel safe and happy enough to want to get married, but I'd very much like to marry you, Bastien Miller, if that's something you'd be interested in."

They were on a plane to Nevada the next morning.

Had dealing with Anais's wedding planning stress inspired what was one of his most impulsive and selfish ideas? Probably. But more importantly, he didn't want Gabby to doubt for a single day that he wanted forever with her, that he would always be there for her.

The thought of his family's surprise was just a bonus. While it would have been nice to have them come, there'd be time for a family celebration later, big or small, whatever they wanted. The day itself, the words full of love spoken in a small chapel in the middle of the night, was something Bastien didn't want to share with anyone other than Gabby.

"Ready?" He gave her another kiss, just because. This one was firmer, deeper, and lasted longer, threatening to derail their entire night.

She pulled away from him with visible effort. "Maybe we can tell them tomorrow..." With a tug of his hand, she took a step backward.

"There you two are!"

They both groaned at the sound of Clementine's voice and turned to see her outlined in the open front door.

Gabby put her head on his shoulder. "Time to see the in-laws."

"Time to see your family."

There was the sharp snap of her inhale, and he felt her relax against him. They walked through the door together, hand in hand, the way he knew they always would.

AUTHOR'S NOTE

Whenever I read a romance novel, I always wonder what's real and what's not.

Yes, I realize the entire point of fiction is that it's made up. But there are always hints of real places, people, and events tucked in between the imaginary dialogue uttered by inexplicably buff and beautiful characters.

This book has one of the most painful backstories I've ever had to create, and I struggled with how much to include. In the end, I chose to touch on some things in Gabby's past that are the reality for many people in the world (drug use by parents and sibling, homelessness), but I don't go into great detail, keeping the focus on Gabby's present and future. Her past is in the past and while it influences her choices, it doesn't define her. Though my story is very different from Gabby's, focusing on the future is how I've chosen to deal with past trauma in my own life. Like Gabby, I've been lucky enough to find people who make me feel safe and loved, and am living my HEA.

On a more lighthearted note, here's a short and incomplete list of other things that are real and not real in this book:

- Jasper Creek, Colorado: not a real town, unfortunately. It sounds like a nice place to live though, doesn't it? So many fun town festivals!
- A bar that makes their own ice cream and beer like the Floodline: sort of real. Lots of places sell boozy milkshakes, or alcohol-infused ice cream. Here's a list, let me know if you've tried one of them!
- Gabby's gastrointestinal issues: real (ish). These were very much inspired by my own struggles and frustration with doctors not being able to identify the problem. I'm happy to say things are much better now than they were a year ago.

MORE SWEET CONTEMPORARY ROMANCE

Want more sweet romance? Take a peek at *Houseplants &*
Hardcovers, a sweet rivals-to-lovers romance with major *You've Got*
Mail vibes and tons of plant puns.

Chapter 1

NOVEMBER

> **JCEdits**
> Hi! Sorry for the random DM. You've been super
> helpful in the comments, but my current plant
> situation has gotten overwhelming.

> **Plantsguy95**
> What seems to be the problem? What kind of
> plants are they?

> **JCEdits**
> Well . . . everything is very, very brown. And they are all, um, green plants? My mother got them for me.

> **Plantsguy95**
> No worries, happy to help with any and all plant problems.

> We'll figure out how to get things back in the green in no time.

APRIL

Pete the prayer plant was dying.

If Juliet was being honest with herself, he had been dying for a while. Then she'd gone into one of her super-concentrated work sprints and did nothing but sleep and copyedit for four days. Now most of her plants looked less than well-loved, sagging sadly over the edge of their pots between teetering stacks of books, but poor Pete had suffered the worst.

Juliet leaned in, examining his leaves in the sunlight streaming through her home office's windows. Unlike Pete, Juliet had gotten some nourishment this week, but only because her mom had sent food over. Almost twenty years since she left home, she still regularly needed to be watered and fed by someone else.

A buzzing from her desk drew her attention away from her plants. Her phone was ringing. She didn't have to look to know it was her mom. No one else called her.

"Did you get the salad?"

"Hello to you too." Juliet tucked the blanket she was wearing over her shoulders even tighter so it draped behind her like a cape. "Yes, I got it."

"Did you eat it?"

"Yes." Not immediately, but within twelve hours. That counted as the same meal, didn't it?

Her mother sighed, as if she'd guessed at Juliet's unspoken words. "It shouldn't be this hard to keep my thirty-seven-year-old daughter alive." The sounds of nature chirped through the phone, along with the babble of a toddler. "Your sister doesn't need this kind of attention. Her small children do."

"So stop sending the salads. I can take care of myself."

"You can't even keep those plants alive."

Juliet had no argument there. Here she was, staring at five shriveled brown leaves on a prayer plant that looked like it was praying to be put out of its misery.

"The plants were your idea. You should be the one to take care of them." The bitterness in her words got another sigh from her mother. Like she needed another reminder about how incompetent she was at managing her own life.

"I water them every time I come over. Or rather, whenever you let me come over."

The itch to get back to her computer and escape this conversation was a thousand writhing ants crawling up her arms. In front of a page, with stylistic errors and typos to be corrected, Juliet was in total control. When online reputations and major financial deals could be ruined forever from a misplaced comma, nothing was more important than the right editor. Her clients' only concern was that she got their manuscripts polished to perfection in record time. They didn't care if she could keep a plant alive.

Juliet tugged gently at the brownest of Pete's leaves, and it slipped off the stem as if attached by only the flimsiest of threads. The prayer plant needed her more than her clients right now, it seemed.

Thank goodness her mother hadn't bought her a cat.

"You can come over tonight, if you want," Juliet said, turning away from Pete to look at the calendar above her desk. "I just finished a deadline, so I don't have much work for the next few days."

"It'll have to wait, sweetie, Allison needs me to watch the boys overnight."

The sting of rejection shouldn't be as sharp after all these years, but there it was. Her mother complained Juliet never wanted her to come over, but then was too busy when she did invite her. Juliet took a deep breath and the pain in her chest eased a bit, though not completely.

"Well, whenever you have time. I'm always here," she said.

"That's what worries me the most. You should get out of the house more."

"Mom, I work at home."

"Exactly. You live your whole life inside." There was a loud squawk from her mother's end of the phone—one of the kids must have seen a dog or something. "Allison's husband just finished his third Ironman this weekend. He almost qualified for the world championships."

"I know. I saw the pictures." Juliet plopped down in her office chair, curled her legs to her chest, and pulled the blanket over herself.

"You could have seen it in person."

"I had a deadline." Also, it had been a three-hour drive to the mountain town to Tony's race. There was no way she would have been able to do that, even if she still had a car.

"I would have driven you." Again, it was as if her mom had guessed the words she'd held back.

Now if only she could pick up on Juliet's desire to get off the phone and back to her plant disaster.

"Next time. I have to go. I'll call you in a few days."

After saying their goodbyes, Juliet hung up and stood up, the blanket dropping to the floor. Rather than deal with the emotions a five-minute phone call had dredged up, she switched to her camera to take a picture of the dying plant. Then, it was just another swipe of her thumb and a few taps of her fingers to pull open the social media app where normally she'd post about the open space in her editing calendar. Instead, she went into the private-messaging section to send the photo to the one person who could help her right now.

Plantsguy95.

There was already a message waiting for her, a laughing emoji in response to a meme she'd sent him a few days ago. From that initial message a few months ago—when her mother had dropped off five plants and they'd all been drooping within a week—an easy online friendship had blossomed.

Blossomed. She almost groaned out loud at the plant pun. That was undoubtedly his influence. He was funny with words in a way she could never achieve without hours of contemplation first.

The little green dot next to his profile picture—a leafy green *Ficus*—let Juliet know he was online. A reply came almost immediately to her picture of a dying Pete.

> **Plantsguy95**
> What happened?

> **JCEdits**
> I got busy with work.

> **Plantsguy95**
> Isn't this one in the bathroom like I suggested, for the humidity?

> Did you not go to the bathroom for a week?

> **JCEdits**
> I plead the fifth.

> **Plantsguy95**
> JC, you gotta be nicer to your body. Forget about the plants.

Juliet snorted. Though it went against all sorts of best practices for using social media to grow your business, she didn't share her name unless someone was a client. Plantsguy95 only knew her as JCEdits, her username, which he turned into JC.

> **JCEdits**
> I'm screenshotting that and showing all your 15 million followers you said that.

> **Plantsguy95**
> 15 million?

> Wow, it must have gone up by 14.99 million since yesterday.

> **JCEdits**
> You mean you don't check your followers?

> You have like, five times as many as me, and people share your stuff all the time.

> **Plantsguy95**
> This isn't my full-time gig.

> It's not even a gig. I don't get paid for this.

> I just want people to learn about plants.

For someone with close to twenty thousand followers, Plantsguy95 had a very laid-back approach to his account that Juliet couldn't understand. Not for the first time, she wondered what his real job was . . . and his name. Neither of them posted pictures of themselves, so she didn't even know what he looked like. All his photos were plants, sometimes with hands she assumed were his, sometimes his shadow. Her account was entirely copyediting tips and memes, her profile photo a stylized red pen.

She knew he was a *he* from the pronouns in his bio, but beyond that, it was frustratingly bare bones, even more anonymous than Juliet's. At least hers told the world what she did and how to contact her. All his said was "I'm a guy who likes plants. I answer your #solvemyplantproblem questions every Wednesday." No location, no link to a website or even a fundraising campaign.

> **JCEdits**
> Thank goodness you aren't trying to get paid for this.

> The sloppy copy in your posts would make any legitimate sponsors run for the hills.

> **Plantsguy95**
> Well, you refuse to let me hire you, so I'll just have to struggle along without your expert eyes.

> **JCEdits**
> Can I get your expert eyes on my plant please?

> I'll write five posts for free for you if it lives to next week.

> **Plantsguy95**
> Deal.

Juliet never took social media clients, since she charged by word, and it was not the most efficient use of her time. This was a dire situation, however, and exceptions had to be made. Within minutes, he sent a comprehensive list of everything Juliet needed to do, almost hour by hour, to make sure Pete survived. The tension that had built up over the last four days dropped off Juliet's shoulders. It was reassuring to see something so organized. Now that she felt like the plant part of her life was under control, she could get back to work.

———

Lucas was in the middle of his shift at the hardware store when he got an update from JC about the prayer plant she'd ignored into drought. It was still drooping a week after he'd told her how to save it, but "since it's technically still alive," she said he could send her the posts he wanted her to write.

His lips curved up into a smile wider than the hacksaws he was pricing as he tapped out a reply.

> **Plantsguy95**
> Are you sure your prayer plant doesn't have a death wish?

JCEdits
The thought has crossed my mind. I thought I was a good roommate.

No complaints from the others, though.

> **Plantsguy95**
> How many others do you have?

JCEdits
Roommates or plants?

> **Plantsguy95**
> I already know how many plants you have, since I've had to keep them all from dying from lack of attention.

JCEdits
And how many is that?

> **Plantsguy95**
> 10.

JCEdits
Ha! I have 12 plants.

I kept the Aloe plants alive all by myself.

> **Plantsguy95**
> I'm positively bursting with pride.

JCEdits
Don't get too proud, you haven't saved the prayer plant yet.

She'd avoided the roommate question, and while it might not

have been intentional, it did remind him that she wasn't that kind of online friend. Personal details shared were minimal. They never talked much about family or friends. She only mentioned her work when it got in the way of her plant care.

Leaning against a shelf full of boxes of nails, Lucas ran a hand through his hair and stared down at his phone, like he could hypnotize it into giving him the information he wanted.

The internet was an amazing thing. You could look up the answers to literally any question, as Lucas liked to remind his family when they blew up his phone with their bonkers requests at three in the morning. Though at least his grandmother waited until the sun was up.

The internet, however, could not solve the question he'd been wondering about for months, despite the embarrassing amount of hours he'd spent sleuthing.

Who was JCEdits?

All he knew for sure was that she was an editor. A few years ago, he would have traded all his plant advice until the end of time to get professionally written and edited posts. What had started as a failed side hustle had turned into an unexpected way to connect with other plant nerds outside of his small town. It wasn't to make money or get famous, at least not anymore. Not since his ex—and his reason for starting the account—was no longer in the picture. Now, he just wanted to talk to people about plants and help them learn more about them.

A few short months ago, JC had been completely clueless. Even worse than his cousin Marigold—Mari—who'd managed to kill a cactus in two days by mixing up the saltwater she'd put in a bottle for her facial routine with . . . well, it didn't really matter since he'd told her at least five times succulents don't need daily watering.

JC was a quick learner though. Since Lucas loved nothing more than people who asked him questions about the things he loved most, they'd been chatting a few times a week since her first timid message asking for help with her brand-new plant babies.

It was nice, in a way, to have something that was light and low pressure. The opposite of his life with a huge family that lived and breathed drama like they were trying out to be the next reality TV sensation.

And yet . . . he really wanted to know if JC lived with anyone.

Instead of asking again, he looked up from his phone to make sure he was still alone in the aisle, and focused his response to her on the plants, like he was expected to.

> **Plantsguy95**
> Why don't you try your local horticultural society?

> **JCEdits**
> I'm sorry, my local what now?

> This isn't the 1800s and I am not a romance heroine with nothing to do until an appropriate suitor comes to call.

> **Plantsguy95**
> Fine, garden club, if you prefer.

> **JCEdits**
> Also not a 1950s housewife waiting for her husband to come home to beat him over the head with a leg of lamb.

He chuckled, and the noise caught his boss's attention. Normally, Henry didn't care about phone use during work. But whenever Henry's dad, who owned the store, was around, the rules suddenly became stricter. So Lucas stashed his phone in his back pocket and got back to pricing boxes of nails under Henry's watchful eye. It was an agonizing three hours before Lucas could reply to JC's message.

His shift finally over, Lucas practically threw his apron at Henry and ran out of the hardware store, passing a row of smaller shops on his way to the back parking lot that employees used. The evening was warm for early spring, and he inhaled a lungful of crisp air as he leaned against the side of his truck and thought about what to tell JC. It was a fine line to walk between revealing too much about himself and coming off as insincere.

The choice to never show his face in the account kept him anonymous. Plants were his main focus on the account, not making it his identity, his business, his life. That hadn't gone very well the first time he'd tried it, as the harsh criticisms of his ex had so generously pointed out.

Besides, Greenhaven was on the smaller side. Five square miles with an adorable store-lined, cobblestone main street that would make Norman Rockwell proud, and a gossip mill that put Hollywood tabloids to shame. Lucas knew word would get around if he put his face out there, then *everyone* would have something to say about it. It was enough trouble as it was to have his younger cousins weigh in on his very outdated use of hashtags.

Now, however, he wished he could tell JC about the garden club in Greenhaven that he'd belonged to since he was old enough to hold a spade.

> **Plantsguy95**
> Google the name of your city + horticultural society or garden club, to see what comes up.

> Most cities of a certain size have one, even if it's just a few people who get together to trade seeds.

> **JCEdits**
> "Trade seeds" huh?

> Is that what the kids these days are calling it?

He laughed out loud at that one, then looked around to make sure no one had seen him. Laughing to himself in a deserted parking lot behind Main Street wasn't exactly his best look. Not to mention if Henry spotted him, he'd probably assume Lucas had nowhere to be tonight and ask him to work a few more hours.

Before he could forget, he drafted a post on garden clubs to share with his followers, giving a bit of the history and importance that they served in communities. It took an enormous amount of restraint to not add anything specific to his town, since he honestly thought they were one of the best in his area. The work they did in Greenhaven was incredible, and not just because his family had done so much of it.

Now dangerously close to having Henry come out and ask him to help close the store, Lucas got into his truck—even years after he passed, it was still hard to not think of it as his grandfather's old truck—to drive to his grandmother's house. On his way, he passed town hall, where the rows of planters were fresh and colorful thanks to the club. Two people chatted away on the nearby bench as the sky turned darker, oblivious to the months of fundraising the garden club had done to get it installed.

Typical. He sighed as he turned onto a side street. *No one appreciates a really good garden.*

There was a family crossing the street to the library, which was lit up inside for some evening event, and Lucas stopped the truck to let them pass. A few buildings down, his cousin Sage's car was parked in front of the garden club, and a light was on.

Their grandmother was still the elected president of the Greenhaven Garden Club, but she'd gotten sick over the winter. Then her best friend had died, and Granny just didn't seem to like being out and about as much. They'd scheduled an election for the next meeting to select an acting president, but for now, the other members rotated duties.

Except Sage wasn't technically a member. She was family, and the Geis family helped each other no matter what. So without a second's hesitation, Lucas pulled into the driveway behind her car, whatever plans he'd had for the evening put on hold in favor of something much more important.

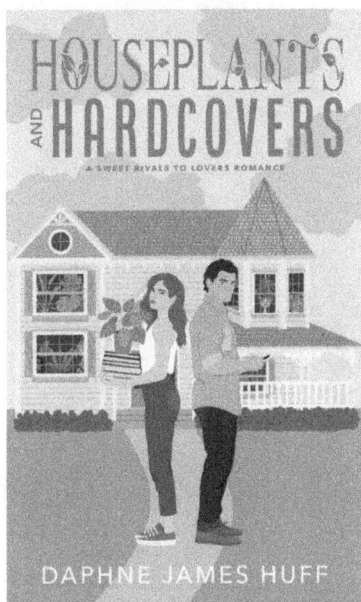

HOUSEPLANTS and HARDCOVERS

A SWEET RIVALS TO LOVERS ROMANCE

DAPHNE JAMES HUFF

ALSO BY DAPHNE JAMES HUFF

Sweet Adult Contemporary Romance:

Houseplants and Hardcovers

Man Of My Dreams

Miller Family Medical:

A Shot At Love

Wrapped Up In You

Braced For Heartache

Wedding Games:

The Bridesmaid and the Reality Show

The Bridesmaid and the Ex

The Bridesmaid and Her Surprise Love

Free Wedding Games Prequel Novella:

The Wedding Planner's Second Chance At Love

ABOUT THE AUTHOR

Daphne James Huff has been writing romance for adult and YA audiences since she was a young adult herself. Her favorite kind of story has a main character who thinks they've got it all figured out until someone barges into their life and messes everything up. She never says no to free cake or cheese, and can usually be found eating both to stay awake after reading all night.

Follow her on Instagram **@daphnejameshuff**

Printed in the USA
CPSIA information can be obtained
at www.ICGtesting.com
LVHW042052050924
789970LV00003B/279

9 798987 725931